JOY'S CHRISTMAS ESCAPE

THE MARSHAL'S MAIL ORDER BRIDE

P. CREEDEN

Sign up for my newsletter to receive information about
new releases, contests and giveaways.
http://subscribepage.com/pcreedenbooks

JOY'S CHRISTMAS ESCAPE

THE MARSHAL'S MAIL ORDER BRIDE ~ Eight brides each find themselves in a compromising situation – and the only way out is to escape west and become a mail-order bride. But will trouble follow them? Good thing they are heading into the arms of a law man. Each bride has a different, standalone story ~ Read all 8 and don't miss out!

JOY'S CHRISTMAS ESCAPE

With danger and redemption swirling around them, can an unlikely Christmas miracle still be found in Virginia City?

Schoolteacher Joy Stewart has never been lucky. Her father died before she was born. Her mother left her in the care of her grandmother so that she could get remarried and move far away. So, when her grandmother succumbs to illness, debtors come to call. And one of them has his eyes set on Joy to be his mistress as payment for the debt. That bad luck just seems to be compounding on Joy—what she needs is a Christmas Miracle, and her grandmother has put a plan in the works...

Marshal Jack Bolling has found himself in want of a nanny. With the death of his sister and her husband in a tragic accident, he has now come into possession of his twin niece and nephew of four years old. For over a month he's had no luck in locating an appropriate nanny for them—at least not on his salary and what a marshal can afford. But then his good friend, Pastor North has the idea that perhaps Jack should be looking for a wife instead? The thought of that sends chills down Jack's spine, but when he ends up putting the twins' lives in danger due to his job, he wonders what choice he has. But can he even dare to hope that he'd be lucky enough to find a wife so close to Christmastime?

CHAPTER 1

"What's that over there?" Sam the barber asked, pointing toward the east.

A storm had just passed over, and Marshal Jack Bolling had been looking west, toward the sunset where the sky was already brightening for the moments just before sunset. The slightest drizzle still hung in the air, dripping a drop or two now and then. But following Sam's question, he looked the direction the man pointed.

Against the still stormy sky, a dark column of smoke rose, darker than the clouds above it. He frowned. "Looks like a fire."

He picked up a jog and headed toward the livery, calling over his shoulder, "Get the men of town together. We may be needing a bucket brigade."

"You bet!" Sam yelled back.

Jack knew he could count on Sam to get most of the men in town on board to help. No one wanted a fire to spread. He couldn't pinpoint exactly where the fire was, but he imagined that it was a bit outside of Virginia City, possibly in one of the farm homes nearby. When he reached the livery, he hollered inside. "Clyde! Grab as many buckets as you can. There's a fire!"

Clyde came out of a horse's stall with a pitchfork, his eyes wide. "Which way?'

"East," Jack answered, as he stepped to the paddock just outside the livery and grabbed hold of his chestnut gelding, Red. Quickly, he swung a saddle on the horse's back and cinched the girth loosely. No matter what kind of hurry he was in, Jack had a promise to keep with Red. He'd never tighten the cinch too fast and would always give the gelding time to adjust before pulling the leather strap hard. He then reached over the horse's head and pulled the bridle up over his ears. Once it was buckled in place, Jack led Red forward a couple of steps before pulling the cinch strap tight. He tied it in its knot and then shoved a foot into the stirrup and swung into the saddle. Before he was all the way up, Red was already moving forward, seeming to sense the urgency in Jack's movements.

Once in the saddle, Jack reined the horse to the east. He didn't know how long Red had been sitting since he'd dropped him off at the livery a couple hours before the storm came. Early October storms still had remnants of the power of those in the late summer. Fall couldn't come soon enough. He was sick of the hail and lightning. He huffed. It might've been lightning that caused this fire. Even as he started letting his gelding jog in the direction of the smoke, he sent up a quick, silent prayer that no one would be hurt.

The cloud over the black column was already thick and wide and continuing to spread. It was worrisome to see the clouds like that. Likely it meant that the fire had been raging for at least a little while. But no one would have noticed because the storm had kept everyone inside. Jack himself had been in the barber shop getting a shave to pass the time while he waited out whatever the storm would bring.

There hadn't been a lot of rain in this one, but the hail had been about dime-sized and the thunder had rumbled for at least an hour. He thought back to the one big crack that had shaken the building about forty-five minutes ago and suddenly he wondered if this fire might have been the result of the lightning that had caused that peal. After a short bit, his horse picked up a lope. He rounded the bend and in the distance it was becoming easier to determine exactly where the fire might be coming from. And immediately his heart sank.

The lope became a gallop as he opened Red up and asked him to move faster. The smoke was coming from a location much too close to his old family home—his sister's house. Another prayer went up as he groaned. No. Please don't let her be hurt. Or the twins. The two cherub faces flashed before his mind as his stomach squeezed, and he felt a little nauseous.

Unfortunately, the closer he got to the fire, the more certain it seemed that it was coming from Penelope and her family's house. As he galloped closer, he found a small crowd of neighbors already trying to form a bucket brigade from the well to the house, but there were only a few of them. A measure of relief hit Jack when he saw his little niece and nephew standing together in their nightgowns with a young woman. They were safe. Thank the Lord.

He ran straight for them, pulling up his horse

when he was a few yards away and launching himself from the saddle. "Penelope!"

The young woman stood and turned about, and that's when he realized the young woman wasn't his sister, it was Grace Scott from across the street. He blinked, his pace faltering for a moment as he took in more of his surroundings. It was then he noticed two bodies that had been covered by blankets nearby. And the world tilted and spun as Grace started speaking to him, but for the ringing in his ears, he couldn't hear a word she said.

DRESSED IN BLACK, JOY STOOD BEFORE A FRESHLY DUG grave, watching as the gravediggers began shoveling in the dirt that would bury her beloved grandmother. How could it be so sunny out when the only family that Joy had in the world—the only person who'd ever loved her—was being buried? Geese flew overhead making such a racket in their migrations, that Joy's own sobs were drowned out. The late October breeze blew in the treetops, sending multicolored leaves to swirl around her and the gravesite.

In the past, Joy had always loved the fall. It was a blessed respite from the hot summers in Memphis.

It was when school started for the children, and when Joy had the most hope for the coming school year. But that had been shadowed by the illness that plagued her grandmother over the last few months. Even though her grandmother had told her that everything was all right and that she should continue to go to the schoolhouse and work, Joy had known better. She regretted listening to her grandmother's pretense. Instead of starting the school year, she should have stayed at home and taken care of her grandmother. Maybe then, her grandmother wouldn't have died so soon. Maybe then, Joy would have been able to take care of her and spend more time with her at least. But she knew that she couldn't have given up the income from teaching at the school. Modest though it was, it helped pay for the medicine to keep her grandmother from the pains she had.

"Miss Stewart," a deep, gruff voice said from behind her.

Swiping at the tears on her cheeks, she turned around, preparing to give a false smile to whoever might be waiting to give her their condolences. But instead, she found a man who was standing much closer to her than she'd expected, a taller, larger man than she'd ever seen before, and she had to tilt her neck back just to meet gazes with him. She furrowed her brow in confusion. "Um... yes. I'm Miss Stewart."

He nodded, taking hold of her elbow. "I knew as much. Come with me, please."

Immediately he started guiding her away from the gravesite. Although the man had said please, it felt like a platitude. There was no denying the brute. When she grew slow to follow, his grip on her elbow tightened, causing her chest to tighten in fear as well. "Where are you taking me?"

"Just come along."

She swallowed hard, her feet catching her as she almost stumbled. Still, she followed knowing she didn't have much choice but to do as he said. If she tried to stop, the reprobate would likely drag her. They continued to make their way down the hill toward the gravel road that lead out of the yard when a black stagecoach pulled by two dark horses came into view. For some reason, the sight of it caused the hairs on the back of Joy's neck to stand on end. It was as if the grim reaper himself might be hiding behind the dark curtain in the window. Her heart raced in her chest as she was pulled out a halt just outside the door of the carriage.

The brute who had been manhandling her kept a hand on her elbow but stepped forward and knocked on the side of the carriage. "Mr. Pomeroy, this here is Miss Joy Stewart."

Her stomach began to quiver and even though there was a slight chill in the breeze, she'd begun to perspire. What did these people want with her?

With a quick swish, the curtain on the carriage opened, revealing a balding, spectacled man with beady, black eyes. He looked her up and down and quirked an eyebrow. Then he smiled, showing pronounced bucked teeth that reminded her of a rat or beaver. "So you're the lone heir to Madam Henrietta Stewart?"

Frowning, but feeling only slightly less afraid, Joy refused to answer. What did this man want with her, and how would he know anything about her or her grandmother?

Then the brute at her elbow shook her. "Answer Mr. Pomeroy, woman."

"Now, now, Big Donald. Don't be too rough with the lady, and show her the respect enough to call her miss. After all, she is a schoolteacher, not a saloon girl."

"Yes, sir." The scoundrel lightened his grip on her arm, but only slightly. "Excuse me, Miss, but please answer Mr. Pomeroy."

Joy swallowed hard, unsure of what was going

on. How did this man even know her name, much less her occupation? Why did it seem that this man knew so much about her, but she'd never heard of him or seen him before in her life? What was going on? Her vision crowded with black dots, and she feared she might faint. But she bit the inside of her cheek in desperation to get a hold of herself. The last thing she wanted to do was faint in front of these villains. The pain in her cheek was sharp but bearable, and it helped to scatter the dots that had threatened to take hold of her. Coppery blood trickled upon her tongue, and she managed to regain her composure. Her hands fisted at her sides, and she yanked her elbow from the brute's grip. Anger overwhelmed the fear she'd felt moments before. "What is this all about, sir? Why would this... this ruffian drag me all the way down here to meet with someone I do not know?"

The smile upon the man's lips didn't change, but his eyes flashed a bit with something like amusement. "Are you angry now, Miss Stewart? I apologize for my man's mishandling of you. It was disrespectful. I'll ask that he not lay a hand upon you again, if that will make you happy."

His sudden sweetness was more unnerving than his appearance. She rubbed at her elbow and didn't say anything again. She wasn't certain just how to respond to this man. But his speech did deflate the anger she'd been building.

The stranger shrugged and pushed open the carriage door. Joy had to step backwards to keep the man from invading her space. He placed a bowler upon his head; the felt hat was only a few shades darker than the brown suit that he wore. He stood at eye-level with her, a small, mousy man who seemed to be the opposite of the heathen who'd grabbed her by the elbow before, but somehow more dangerous. Her hair stood on end again while he looked her up and down again, taking measure of her.

Her voice shook as she asked, "Mr. Pomeroy, was it? Could I ask what business you have with me?"

His brow lifted again. "You are a pretty one, aren't you. It shouldn't be surprising. Even as an old crone, you could tell that Ms. Henrietta Stewart was quite the looker back in her day. My father had said as such. It was one of the reasons that he was so quick to give her the loans that she asked for."

Joy frowned. "What loans?"

"What loans?" The man chuckled and shook his head. Then he began pacing around her in a circle. "Surely you're not going to play ignorant with me, are you? I already know that you're not stupid. After all, you are a schoolteacher."

"How... how do you know I'm a schoolteacher," she asked, feeling a bit breathless.

"I make it my business to know as much as I can about those who owe me debts. And since Ms. Henrietta Stewart is now no longer able to pay her debts, the burden, unfortunately is passed on to you, Miss Joy Stewart, as the former's only living heir."

The shiver that had started in Joy's stomach began to quake in earnest. "What... what do you mean? I have no earthly idea what you are talking about." She hated that she couldn't stop the shaking or remove the slight whine out of her voice.

The man stopped directly in front of her, narrowing his beady black eyes and taking her chin in his hand. "Whether you want to play dumb or actually are dumb enough to think that your grandmother could live at the house where you have made your home the last fifteen years without employment or indebtedness, it doesn't matter. The truth of the matter is that your grandmother owes my family two thousand four hundred dollars, and I've come to collect."

CHAPTER 2

Joy's world tilted. Two thousand four hundred dollars? How could that be possible? That was more money than she'd ever seen…ever heard of. Those spots that had crowded her vision before circled around her in earnest. They were bigger, faster, and laughed at her while threatening to steal her consciousness. She blinked at the mousy man in front of her, instinctively knowing that he was much more dangerous than his appearance seemed. After all, he ordered around the bigger brute at her elbow as though he were the smaller one. She swallowed hard. "How… how can I know this is true? That… that my grandmother honestly owed you the amount you claim?"

Mr. Pomeroy's head tilted and his eyes showed a

modicum of pity, though it looked condescending. "Oh, I have all the paperwork I need to take in front of a judge if you'd rather that I did this the legal, difficult way. Your grandmother signed every one of the papers needed in order to take out the loans. My father deferred her loans as often as he could and even left her alone while she was bedridden. But now that she's gone, I'm afraid that all of those deferments are finished. The money is due."

There was no deceit in the man's words or his tone. She was sure that everything he was saying was true, but still, she needed more time to figure out what he meant by what he was saying. This was all too much. Even as she tried to slow her breathing, she couldn't seem to fill her lungs to capacity. After closing her eyes, she tried harder to pull in a deep breath, but it was impossible. Her heart raced in her chest. Then she opened her eyes, finally succumbing to the fact that she was somehow going to need to pay this debt. "Is it possible for me to get more time? I can sell my grandmother's house and belongings, and give you the proceeds."

The side of the man's lip ticked up in a smirk. "I'm afraid that your grandmother already signed over the house to me, and she already declared all of her valuables. The two thousand four hundred is the remaining debt."

Nausea overcame her for a moment, and she thought she was going to be sick. How much money did her grandmother owe before? And how on earth was Joy going to be able to pay back the debt if she owned nothing of that sort of value. "I... I make a modest income as a schoolteacher. After I afford my living, I can give you all that I have left... if you're willing to allow me to make payments over time."

Slowly, Mr. Pomeroy shook his head and tched his tongue. "I'm afraid that wouldn't even cover the interest on the loan, Miss Stewart."

Tears stung the backs of her eyes as the bluster she'd felt a moment before fled and fear gripped her. Her cheek hurt. How could she possibly pay back the man if the loan was accruing more interest than she could afford on her meager salary. Her mind raced, trying to figure out something that she could do, but at the same time, her body felt suddenly heavy as though it had already given in to the fact that there was nothing she could accomplish in this situation.

"Of course," the man said in a softer voice than he'd used before, stepping closer to her. "We could make other arrangements in order to fulfill your debt. I'm a kind, generous man and could forgive your debt if you were to do favors for me."

As she was just a schoolteacher, what favor could she possibly do for him? Swiping at her eyes as she blinked away her tears, she hugged her shoulders and took a step back, trying to increase the distance between them, but instead, she ended up stepping into the brutish man behind her, Big Donald. "What... what do you mean?" she asked.

He offered a half shrug and stepped into her.

The shiver in her gut intensified as she hugged herself harder. She wanted to back away, but it was impossible with the wall of flesh standing behind her, his hand on her elbow again, proving she had no means of escape.

Mr. Pomeroy leaned toward her, close enough that she could feel his breath upon her cheek, and she closed her eyes and leaned away as much as she could but it was no use. His whisper came to her anyway. "You could become my mistress."

Her stomach lurched, and anger straightened her spine. She opened her eyes and before she could stop herself, she pulled from the brute's hand on her elbow and slapped the smaller man across the face as hard as she could.

His eyes went wide, flashed with anger, surprise,

and then amusement as he stepped back and put a hand to his cheek. The rogue behind her sucked in a sharp breath. But Joy didn't want to give either of the men the opportunity to capture her by the arm again. Quickly she ducked and darted away from them. Afraid to look back and fearing they might chase her, she marched as quickly as she could toward the road and down the street toward the church that wasn't too far away. If she could just make it to the whitewashed building fifty yards away, perhaps she could find sanctuary there.

"My apologies, Miss Stewart," the man behind her called out. "I wasn't meaning to insult an upstanding woman such as yourself." He chuckled, mirthlessly.

That laughter chased her to the doors of the church where she finally looked back toward the carriage to find that both men had disappeared within it and the horses had started away. She held the cold metal handle of the church's door and watched as they left. Some measure of relief came over her. But her breaths still came out heavy and quickly, although her heart finally began to settle. Unfortunately, her stomach remained twisted as the fear remained. What could she possibly do? She was lost. Closing her eyes, she remembered what her grandmother had said before about what any of God's children should do when they were lost. Pray. And with renewed determination, she opened her eyes and pulled upon the door of the church and stepped inside.

Because of the bright sunlight outside, the sanctuary seemed even darker than it actually was, and Joy had to blink several times, leaving her eyes closed for a second extra each time to try to get them used to the darkness. The door behind her closed and once she could see well enough, she moved forward down the row at the center of the church and made her way toward the front. Filtered light came through the opaque windows that sat high on the walls, closer to the ceiling. Lantern light lit the altar and podium that stood at the front. Pastor North sat on the front pew with his head bowed.

Slowly, Joy approached, her footsteps echoing overloud in the silence. She stopped when she was just a couple pews back and bowed her own head in prayer. After thanking the Lord for saving her from what seemed to be becoming a harrowing situation, she asked God for the help needed to do what she could about her grandmother's debt and whatever else she might need to endure over the coming days. When she lifted her head again, she found Paster North had stood and turned toward her.

"Hello, Joy. It's good to see you." He offered her a welcoming smile.

"Pastor," she croaked, suddenly feeling like she needed to swallow down the sobs that were wanting to overtake her.

His brow furrowed, he stepped around the pew and came to her, setting a hand upon her shoulder. "Oh, Joy, don't mourn too heavily. Your grandmother is at Jesus bosom now, I'm sure of it, and you know that a Christian's joy is that the grave cannot defeat us. You'll see her again." He hesitated a moment, then asked, "Is everything else all right?"

She shook her head, not trusting herself to speak. Tears already stung the backs of her eyes, and she was doing all that she could just to keep them at bay. If she let them go, she knew the floodgates would open and then she would just be blubbering in the church. Before she dared to speak, she needed to get control of herself.

But the pastor just nodded knowingly, causing Joy a bit of confusion before he asked, "Is this about Mr. Edgar Pomeroy?"

A gasp escaped her as she widened her eyes.

"I suspected as much. I thought I spotted the villain's carriage among the other mourners."

"How..." was all that she could say before another sob blocked her from speaking.

"Your grandmother told me everything. She told me about the debt, which she'd paid in full, by the way, and how the Pomeroys' were demanding an exorbitant amount of interest. It's all illegal, but unfortunately all three judges in Memphis are on the Pomeroys' payroll. No one will give a debtor a fair hearing about complaints against the Pomeroys. Your grandmother worried that upon her death, they would pressure you into continuing to pay."

She swallowed down the lump in her throat, the feelings of despair leaving her and slowly being replaced by anger. "My grandmother already paid the debt, and yet they are continuing to collect interest?"

He nodded. "It's what they do. Ever since Edgar the third took the reins from his father, he enacted a policy that makes it nearly impossible to clear any debt you owe them. The only way is to pay the amount in full, but for most that is an unlikely occurrence."

"It's unfair!"

"Grossly. But the lawmen around here and the

judges are unlikely to act upon him. Which is why your grandmother has been in touch with a woman who could help hide you as far from the Pomeroys' grasp as possible."

Hope blossomed in her chest. "How?"

"She's been in correspondence with a matchmaker in Denver, Colorado. If you're willing, you could become a mail-order bride and escape Memphis."

That hope that had blossomed just a moment before was snuffed out immediately. Her heart sunk. Married? And leave Memphis? How could she do either one and abandon the children she taught? No, that couldn't be the answer. There had to be another way.

MARSHAL JACK BOLLING'S ELDERLY MOTHER HADN'T taken the news of her daughter's death well, at all. Shucks, he hadn't taken it well either. His heart ached in his chest and he felt empty, truly empty within himself. Penelope had been nearly ten years younger than Jack. She was their miracle baby—one that their parents had long after they thought they couldn't have another. Jack's mother had been a spinster, and hadn't been married until she was twenty six. Soon after, they had Jack, but it seemed a second child wasn't in their cards until Penelope came as a surprise. She was their father's pride and joy until he passed away just before the birth of his sister's twins. Penelope had often said that even though he was sick, she was just happy he'd been there to walk her down the aisle on her wedding day.

Penelope was more than a little sister to Jack, too. He babied and loved her almost as much as his parents did. Her husband had had a hard time courting Penelope because Jack was so over-protective. But eventually, things went the right way, and Jack had loved the birth of his niece and nephew and found them both to be the biggest blessing.

Now Penelope and her husband were gone. And those two angelic twins were with Jack and his mother who was little more than bedridden. He sighed as he stepped out of the kitchen and into the living room of the apartment above the jailhouse in Virginia City just in time to catch little Nathan and stop him from tripping over the rug which had gotten a bulge in it from their constant play.

There had been hardly enough space for him and his mother in the two-bedroom loft, but now that they had the twins running around, he realized that it was a much smaller area than he'd ever thought of it as before.

"Coffee?" his mother asked as she came into the kitchen.

Jack nodded toward the pot and the mug that sat upon the counter. "I already poured you a mug a short bit ago to let it cool off."

"Thank you, dear," she said as she picked up the mug and limped toward the chair, sitting down gingerly.

Little Natalie jumped up and down at his hip, arms raised saying, "Up! Pick me up too, Uncle Jack."

Unwilling to disappoint, he leaned over and scooped her up with his other arm and set both of the twins upon his hips. They were going to be too heavy before long to be held like this, but for now he could enjoy the moment. His heart sank a bit as he thought about how their father, Harold, must have enjoyed holding the two of them like this as well.

It had been nearly three weeks since the children had lost their parents in the fire. At first, they'd ask for their mother almost constantly and with lots of tears, but slowly they adapted to life as it was now. Children sure could bounce back quickly.

A bell rang downstairs, and Jack frowned.

His mother let out a soft sigh. "It's time to go," she said as she stood, her hands open. "Hand one of them to me."

Jack's frown deepened as he set them both down. He hated how tired his mother looked. She wasn't of the age to be taking care of such young children like this. Grandmothers were supposed to enjoy their grandchildren—spoil them, even—not raise them up entirely. "I'll take them with me for a bit while you get your breakfast. I've already fed them both."

Her hands went to her hips. "What if you're needed desperately down there?"

Taking both the twins by their hands, he started for the stairs. "I'll deal with it when that happens. You just worry about getting a moment to yourself so that you can eat."

She nodded and turned back toward her mug of coffee. "It sure would be nice to have a little help around here."

"I already put out an advertisement for a nanny. I just haven't heard anything back on that regard yet."

She shook her head, and Jack barely heard her mumble under her breath before he slipped done the stairs, "That wasn't quite what I meant."

Though it took the threesome a few extra minutes to make it down the steps, when they reached the bottom landing, they found Virginia City's Baptist minister standing, looking out the barred window at the street outside with his hands behind his back. Jack helped the twins down the last step and then called out a greeting, "Pastor Lamb, what a pleasant surprise. Hopefully you're here on a friendly call and not business?"

The pastor turned toward them with a smile on his face that lit up brighter when he saw the twins. Immediately he knelt down and scooped up the children as they ran into his embrace. "Hello, Nathan and Natalie. How are the both of you?"

Each of them babbled back their answers in their own sweet ways. After listening to them intently, the pastor patted them both upon the head and then stood. He smiled up at Jack. "It's good to see they are both adjusting well."

Jack nodded, a lump forming in his throat.

"Well, I'm not here just for a friendly visit. I was wondering if you'd mind riding with me to look in on Ray Johnson? He's usually a regular attender at the church, but he missed service yesterday. And then this morning, I saw his friend, Charlie, over at the diner, so I asked about Ray. Charlie said that no one has seen him since last Thursday. He was missing in the mine on Friday, and that means he missed payday. It's unlike a miner to ever miss his pay."

Frowning, Jack nodded. "Ray Johnson is the one that lives out on the mountain pass, right? Rides his cart in and picks up others along the way? What of them? Have they not seen him either?"

"Charlie is one of those that usually caught a ride with Ray. According to him, Ray just didn't show up. He and the others were late on Friday and had to get up earlier and walk their way down the mountain this morning. Thursday afternoon is the last anyone's seen of him."

This didn't sound good. "I'll ride up there directly with you," he said. Then turning to the twins who had been playing with the items on his desk, he continued, "Let's get you back upstairs to Grandma, all right?"

The wide-eyed cherubs nodded, and then Nathan cried, "I bet you can't beat me up the stairs," and took off at a lick.

"Not fair! You got a head start," Natalie yelled back as she ran after her brother.

"Careful, you two!" Jack called after them, knowing that his words were futile as he heard the two of them pounding up the steps, sounding heavier than grown men. He shook his head at them.

"So, how goes the search for a nanny?" the pastor asked from behind him.

Jack frowned, his heart sinking a bit in his chest. He turned back toward the preacher. "Not well, I'm afraid. I've sent a letter in to a nanny agency down in Denver, but she replied back that she'd have no interest in 'sending an unwed lady up to a mining town with a reputation like Virginia City's to live on such a modest sum in squalor.'" He sighed. "So, I've sent a letter out to another agency in Chicago, hoping for a better result."

Shaking his head, Pastor Lamb put a hand to his chin. "Perhaps you are looking at this all wrong. Maybe you shouldn't be writing to an agency to procure a nanny."

Scrunching his brows, Jack asked, "What do you mean?"

After he shrugged, the pastor said, "Maybe instead of a nanny, you should be in search of a wife?"

Jack's heart skipped a beat and he flushed. Shaking his head, he waved off the idea. "Oh no, I couldn't do that. I couldn't ask a woman to marry into this kind of life—to a lawman who would be gone to work for the town constantly, to take care of two children that aren't hers and a sickly mother-in-law... not to mention, I'm not the most handsome of men or most eligible of bachelors. I'm already thirty. There are plenty of better men in Virginia City who could woo a bride with courting and such, but I'm certainly not that kind."

The pastor looked him up and down. "There's nothing wrong with you. You're a healthy, Christian man. Why do you feel that you couldn't woo a bride?"

Frowning, Jack shook his head. "I'm not a smart man—and women, they're the most difficult math problem any man has ever had to figure out."

A laugh burst forth from the pastor as he set a hand on Jack's shoulder. "Isn't that the truth. Still, you might consider it. Your mother's strength won't stand up to those two four-year-olds for long, and you're not able keep watch over the town as marshal while also running after the twins. A nanny seems like what you want, but it's hard to afford a good one even if your ability to offer a better salary were there. I think it's not about what you want, Jack, but what you need."

Still, Jack shook his head. "I'll just wait until I get word back from Chicago."

Releasing a sigh, the pastor nodded. "All right, but if you don't get back a good word, at least consider what I've said. And pray on it. I really believe that this is what God's plan is for you."

Jack swallowed hard and put a hand on the banister, ready to escape the thoughts that the pastor was putting into his head. He really hoped that it wasn't God's plan for him to be a burden to some poor, unsuspecting lady out there. He cleared his throat, determined to change the subject. "I'll be right back. Just going to tell mother where I'm off to and then I'll be ready to go with you to check on Ray." And then before anyone could say anything else that Jack might regret hearing, he dashed up the steps like he was racing against something himself.

CHAPTER 3

For over a week, Joy had been looking over her shoulder and jumping at every bump while she was alone in her grandmother's house. She'd even taken to sleeping with her grandfather's hunting rifle next to her bed. What was she so afraid of? Memories of the beady-eyed Mr. Pomeroy and his large ruffian, Big Donald, plagued her. It was as if they might hide in one of her closets and jump out at her at any moment. Shaking her head while she ran a brush through her hair, she met eyes with herself in the mirror. "You're stronger than this, Joy Stewart. And you won't let those villains push you around. God is your refuge and strength and your ever-present help in times of trouble."

Then she let out a slow breath. Psalm 46 had

been a blessing to her, and she'd been saying it to herself whenever the fear felt as though it might overtake her. That one, and Joshua 1:9, which she said to herself before standing, "for the Lord your God will be with you wherever you go."

It made her feel much better and helped her put one foot in front of the other whenever her joints felt frozen in trepidation. After meeting her eyes once more in the mirror, Joy turned around and took hold of her bonnet, tying it beneath her chin before making determined steps out the door of the house and down the street, refusing to look behind her to see if she were being followed although that constant apprehension trod on her heels each step of the way. Then she rounded the bend and looked up, only to find that everything she feared wasn't behind her after all. In front of her was the very carriage of death and dread she thought was following her.

She froze in her tracks and for a moment considered turning around and running the other direction. But where would she go? The blasted carriage was parked in front of the schoolhouse. Even though it would be nearly an hour before any of the children arrived, she had duties to attend to. Saying a quick, silent prayer, she forced herself to walk forward and continue toward the school. But as she drew closer, she realized that the two villains she had misgivings about being in the carriage were actually speaking to the schoolmaster. Her eyes widened as butterflies danced in her stomach. Even as she approached cautiously, the schoolmaster spotted her and met her gaze.

Blinking and somehow managing a smile, she called, "Good morning, Mr. Clemons."

But the man didn't return her greeting or smile. He shook his head, brow furrowed. And then said something to the two ruffians as they nodded their goodbyes and started mounting the carriage once more. Mr. Pomeroy met eyes with her and tipped his hat her direction with a grin before disappearing into the black-as-night carriage. Some measure of relief came over her as it pulled away quickly. She let out a sigh as stepped up to the schoolmaster feeling her chest tighten at his morose expression.

Confused, she wanted to ask what the matter was, but was afraid to speak.

The man lifted his chin and cleared his throat. "I'm sorry to hear that you've fallen upon hard times, but it is no excuse for untoward behavior. It has come to my attention that you have been participating in activities that are unbecoming of a schoolteacher at this facility. Therefore, I am forced to ask for your resignation."

The relief she'd felt just a moment before was gone in an instant, replaced by sorrow but also indignation at the injustice. "I have no earthly idea what you are referring to. If that man... Mr. Pomeroy has spoken against me, I assure you, he is a liar."

Anger flashed in the schoolmaster's eyes. "How dare you speak against one of the biggest benefactors of our school? Mr. Pomeroy is an upstanding citizen and a pillar of the community here in Memphis. He would not stoop to spreading gossip or lying, as you accuse him. He was only here a moment ago because I called him to see if he could help us advertise for a new schoolteacher since we'd be letting one go. Neither of us mentioned you by name. I am simply responding to the overwhelming complaints that we have received from the parents' association. They are the ones demanding that we do something about the miscreant in our midst."

Miscreant? Was the schoolmaster actually implying that she was a malefactor? She shook her head. "But I've done nothing wrong. Whatever it is that the parents' association has said that I've done, I haven't. In fact, I honestly do not know what they even possibly could have said."

The schoolmaster gave her a look that spoke volumes about his unbelief. "Every wrongdoer demands their innocence, but we have several who have come forward as witnesses against your acts, so there's no need to perjure yourself further. We have all the evidence we need to remove you from your position. So please, act quickly and remove any personal items from the schoolhouse before the children begin to arrive. I will be teaching your class, myself, until a suitable replacement has been found."

Her heart sank in her chest, and she just stared at the schoolmaster for a moment. Could this truly be happening? How could witnesses have come forward for something that she'd never done? What did they even claim that she had done exactly? How could she fight against something invisible and unknown? She prayed again for help from God, while tears stung the backs of her eyes. Lifting her eyes, she tried to swallow them back.

The schoolmaster sighed impatiently.

Steeling herself, Joy stepped forward and entered the schoolhouse, immediately looking around to see if there was anything she needed to retrieve.

JACK BLEW OUT A BREATH, AND IT CLOUDED AROUND his face. His shoulders shrugged, trying to get the collar of his fleece jacket to cover more of his neck and his chin. So cold. Too cold for this early in November. For the past three weeks, he'd been escorting the pastor up the mountain pass to Ray Johnson's house at least twice a week. When they'd found Ray, he'd had his upper leg broken in a horrific injury, kicked by a mule he was readying Friday morning, and had spent three days on the ground in his barn, dehydrated, and barely surviving. Unfortunately, Ray was a mountain man, a miner with no family and he lived over two miles away from his nearest neighbor. So, if Pastor Lamb hadn't checked up on him, who knew when help would have arrived or if it would have arrived on time?

Little ticks of frozen rain flicked against his felt hat, and he hoped that it wouldn't get any worse. The last thing they needed was an ice storm. At least they were heading back down the mountain instead of up it. The air around them felt heavy and the sky seemed closer—the cloud cover a dilute shade of gray.

The pastor's roan mare walked beside Jack's as they made their way down the gentle slope. "I'll be glad when Ray's back on his feet again," the pastor said, his voice muffled by his own collar. "It's going to be rough going if we're still making this trip and winter comes early."

Jack nodded in his jacket, even though he wasn't sure if the pastor was looking at him. They'd been bringing Ray food and supplies provided by the generous people back in town to help the miner get back on his feet. It brought tears to Ray's eyes that so many of the people in town wanted to help him. Charlie, Ray's nearest neighbor, had even moved into Ray's small house for a few weeks, caring for his animals and making sure that the man was eating and resting properly. It was a testament to the good people of Virginia City that they were willing to work extra to help one of their own. But the pastor was right. If the weather today was any indication, they were possibly looking at an early winter. It wasn't what they needed... now or ever, really.

They passed Charlie's house and saw the small whiffs of smoke that made their way up from the stovepipe at the top of the small shack. Charlie's brother and sister-in-law were taking care of the house in Charlie's stead. The newlyweds didn't yet have a house of their own, so it likely helped that they could get some time together without Charlie around over the past couple weeks. It brought Jack's mind back to what the pastor had suggested a few times, now. Marriage. That Jack should be looking for a wife instead of a nanny. More of his breath crowded his vision as he let out a sigh.

There were so many reasons that he shouldn't look for a wife. He was completely against the idea. But it had been over a month now that he'd been searching for a nanny to no avail. Perhaps if he could find some sort of compromise, he'd be willing to work with. Was it possible to have a wife that didn't have to be completely committed to him? He didn't live the kind of life that was conducive to being a husband. Shoot, he didn't live the kind of life that was conducive to being a father, either, yet he'd had the role thrust upon him because of Penelope's death. The thought of that still made his heart squeeze in his chest. His poor sister. And the poor twins having to live without a mother.

Even though Jack's mother had always been a great influence on the twins, and loved them to pieces, her health wasn't strong, and seemed to be declining since she'd been having to work harder to keep up with the twosome. It wasn't right to ask her to step up and take on the role of mother, too. Occasionally, Pastor Lamb's wife also helped with the twins, but she had three children of her own to take care of, and the last thing that he ever wanted the twins to feel was that they were a burden of any kind. They were not. They were a joy.

When they finally reached the church, Jack nodded a silent goodbye to the pastor. The little flecks of frozen rain had intensified, making Red, Jack's gelding, tuck in his rear end and hold his head down especially low. Jack rode him directly into the livery stable to get cover before dismounting. As soon as Jack was free from the saddle, the gelding did a full body shake, flinging bits of ice in all directions. There were still shards of it stuck in his mane and tail.

"It sure is quiet out there," Mr. Clyde Wheeler, the livery man said as he came up and took hold of Red's reins.

Jack nodded, pulling the gloves from his hands as he uncinched the saddle. "People tend to hunker down inside when there's a storm like this. No one wants to be caught out in it."

"That's for sure. How's Ray?"

"Healing, but impatient. Charlie says he's already trying to hobble around on that broken leg, but you can tell it's still hurting, even though Ray claims it's not."

The livery man took the saddle from Jack after he pulled it from the horse's back. "It's hard for a man to be patient when he's used to doing everything on his own. But that leg is weak, so he needs to stay off it for a few more weeks. Hopefully he'll listen to sense."

"I've a mind to tell on him to the doctor so that he can go out there and talk some sense into him, but honestly I'm not sure it will help," Jack said, shaking his head and replacing his gloves. "Thanks for the assistance."

The livery man nodded and then started leading Red in the direction of the horse's stall, his voice growing louder as he got further away. "It's coming down harder out there, so the way might be slick. Watch your step on the way home!"

After pulling up his collar again, Jack started out into the sleet as it continued to come down like a light rain. Even though it was only six o'clock or so, the lamplighter was already on the street with his pole, stopping at each lantern along the way. It was a good thing, too since with the clouds, it was growing dark early. On his way, Jack slipped once, but didn't do more than lose his footing and start his heart racing. Regardless, he was happy when he'd finally reached the front of the jailhouse. Once inside, he knocked the ice off his boots, hat and jacket, but frowned, as he could still see his breath. No lanterns were lit in the building, and the room was cast in shadows.

Frowning, he called out, "Hello? Mom?"

Pulling off his gloves, he stuffed them into his jacket pockets and then removed his coat. Even in his flannel, the room remained chilly. That wasn't good. He'd started a good fire in both wood stoves before he'd left. Was it possible his mother had forgotten to feed the one downstairs? He lit a lantern, stepped over to the stove and started pushing in wood and paper for kindling before lighting it with a match. But he'd heard nothing but silence from upstairs in the five minutes or so that it had taken him to start the fire going. After shutting the front grate on the stove, he stood and dusted off his hands. Lighting lamps along the way, he called out again before heading up the stairs. "Mom, you there?"

Still, no answer. His stomach twisted. What was wrong? Why wasn't his mother answering? Where were the twins? Perhaps they'd all gone over to a neighbor's house or to the church... He tried to assure himself as he continued up the steps to the second floor. No lamps were lit in the living area either, and the wood was cold. His frown deepened as he started a fire and lit the lanterns in the room as well. It was then that he heard a groan from his mother's bedroom and a faint voice calling his name, "Jack?"

Grabbing one of the lanterns he'd lit, he stepped into the room and found his mother lying upon the floor. His heart sank as he rushed over to her to help her up. "Mother! Are you all right?"

Her skin was cold to the touch everywhere except on her face which burned hot. He helped her to the bed, since she didn't have the strength enough to stand.

"How long have you been on the floor? What's happened?"

She shook her head, a sob coming up although she didn't shed tears. "Water. Could you get me something to drink, please," she asked in a raspy voice.

"Of course," he said as he stepped out of the room quickly and poured a cup from the jug in the kitchen. At least the house had already been warming up. But there were too many unanswered questions. He looked around again, but didn't see a sign of the twins. A tremor shook in his hands as he handed the cup to his mother.

Somehow, it seemed to take an eternity for her to finish the cup. Without meaning to, Jack had begun tapping his foot on the floor impatiently.

"Where are the twins?" he finally asked as she pulled the cup from her lips.

"I'm sorry." His mother shook her head, her expression grave. "I don't know."

His heart sank further in his stomach, and panic started to grip him. "What do you mean? What happened?"

Sadness overcame her features. "I was so tired. So very tired, so I had them lie down with me to take a nap. But somehow as I was asleep, it got so dark. I don't know how long I was asleep. And they were gone, everything was cold and dark and the twins were gone. I fell out of the bed when I tried to get up. I don't understand why I feel so weak and tired."

He felt her forehead again. "You're burning up. It's a fever. That's why you slept so long and why you don't feel well." He cursed inwardly. "Stay here, stay bundled up. The house will be warm shortly."

After he turned on his heel, he marched out of the door. He saw this morning that his mother didn't seem quite right, but he had thought his mother was only tired. Sickness hadn't even entered his thoughts. And he'd left her alone all day with the children. All day. How long had the twins been gone? Where were they gone? And in this ice storm. He cursed himself again. This was entirely his fault. He should have stayed home. What if something happened to the twins? He'd never forgive himself if they weren't okay. Racing down the stairs, he called out their names. "Nathan, Natalie! Are you there? Where are you?"

Silence. No answer.

Had they really gone outside in this storm? Even without the storm, going out of the house in a busy town like Virginia City would be a danger for the two four-year-olds. Tears stung the backs of his eyes as he shoved his arms into the sleeves of his jacket again. He was killing his mother with caring for these young children at her age. And now, if something happened to those two cherubs, he didn't know how he was going to live with himself.

CHAPTER 4

Shoving his hat on his head, Jack rushed out the door. Looking around the immediate parameter of the jailhouse, he called out the twins' names again. "Natalie! Nathan?"

Except for the gentle tick-ticking of the ice hitting the rooftops everything was silent. Panic was overcoming him, and he wasn't sure which direction to go. But still, he knew they were here somewhere. How far could they have gotten without being seen by someone? He rushed down the street calling Natalie and Nathan's names over and over. "Natalie! Nathan!"

Only the hollow wind answered. He fought down panic, glancing in every alley and doorway, praying for a glimpse of two small figures in the quickly gathering darkness. Then he stopped for a moment and just breathed, trying to get a hold of himself. There was no point in blindly running about. He needed help. Closing his eyes, he sent up a prayer, asking the Lord to please keep the children safe until he could find them.

When he opened his eyes again, Jack hurried toward the church. Perhaps they had sought to play with the other children, or at least shelter there? The icy rain pierced Jack's exposed skin like tiny needles as he reached the church building, he banged hard against the church doors until finally, Mrs. Lamb answered her brow furrowed in confusion.

"I'm sorry to bother you folks at a time like this but you haven't seen the twins, have you? They're missing."

Mrs. Lamb paled. "Oh no! No, Marshall Bolling. We haven't seen them all day. In this storm? Are you sure they aren't inside somewhere?"

"I can only hope so," he said as he already started stepping backward down the steps.

"Should I get the pastor? He can help you look for them."

Nodding, Jack said, "That would be great. But don't you get out in this cold, and keep your own children safe, understand?"

"Of course. We'll all be praying for you to find them safe and sound."

"I'm heading down Main Street next. The pastor can find me there," he said as he turned on his heel and started jogging, his boots slipping on the slick roads. The first place with lights on was the general store. Bursting through the door, he scanned the few customers inside but saw no sign of the twins. Breathlessly, Jack asked the shop owner, Mr. Miller if he'd seen either of the twins. The storekeeper shook his head sadly at Jack's breathless inquiry.

Back outside, Jack stood for a moment, the icy rain dripping from the brim of his hat. Where could they be? Could they have wandered up into the nearby foothills or mountains around Virginia City and gotten lost among the trees and mining equipment? Then it struck him—the foothills. The twins loved scrambling over the rocky slopes, playing miners in the scattered abandoned shafts.

"Jack!" Pastor Lamb called out as he jogged down the street and met him in front of the store. "You haven't found them yet?"

Shaking his head, Jack answered, "I'm going to check the foothills and mining area. Their father would let them play there occasionally. Could you continue checking down Main Street? If you find them send word."

The pastor nodded and started toward the next bustling business, the barber shop. Good, perhaps he'd find a few more people that could help with the search, Jack hoped.

Careful of the ice, Jack raced as fast as he dared for the wooded hills looming through the gloom of the storm. Night was almost upon them and everything was covered in ice. The tree limbs that reached toward him shone like crystal as they were encased in almost an inch. Icicles hung down from the larger branches. As Jack shouted the twins' names, the wind howled in macabre laughter. Fighting his way through brush and stumbling over loose shale, Jack scoured every rocky hollow and stand of trees. Just as despair seized him, he heard a faint cry ahead, "Uncle Jack!"

Bursting into a small clearing strewn with mining debris, Jack spotted them. Natalie and Nathan sat huddled together against a lichen-encrusted boulder, soaked and shivering. Sobbing in relief, Jack ran to sweep the twins into his embrace. "Don't worry, I've got you now. You're safe."

Natalie and Nathan clung to him, trembling as Jack hurried back with them through the storm's fury. A prayer of thanks tumbled from his shivering lips into the icy darkness.

"Jack!" Pastor Lamb cried out as Jack made his way back on the main thoroughfare with a twin huddled in each arm. "Thank the Lord. You found them!"

With the pastor were several of the patrons from the saloon, miners most of them, at least a group of ten. One of the miners removed his jacket and put it over top of Natalie. Seeing him do that, another miner did the same for Nathan.

Jack nodded and thanked them both as they all made their way back to the nearest place of warmth, the saloon. Once inside, the bartender had one of the saloon girls grab a blanket for the children. Together a girl helped Jack get the cold children out of their over clothes and set them in front of the fireplace they had there. Normally the business was bustling with gambling, carousing, and singing, but everything remained fairly quiet except for the low buzz of conversation going on in pockets of the room. The pastor brought over two warm mugs of broth. "The bartender made these for the children."

"Oh, thank you so much," Jack said and then nodded an additional thanks toward the barkeep as he took one of the mugs from Pastor Lamb and offered it to Natalie.

The little girl took the mug with a small, quiet word of thanks and then sipped it. "It's warm," she said with a soft sigh.

Nathan's teeth were still chattering as he took his mug. Somehow it seemed that he'd taken the brunt of the cold and was having a harder time adjusting. Jack pulled the boy into his lap hoping that the closeness of their bodies would help the boy get more heat to him. The fire in front of them was doing wonders.

"Is there anything more that I can do?" the saloon girl asked.

Jack recognized her as the one who played the piano. "Is it possible that you could play a tune? Something the children might know?"

A smile spread across the girl's lips. "I think I have just the thing," she said as she turned and walked straight toward the instrument. The girl was dressed in black and red, covered head to toe but in a manner that would still be considered bawdy, but the smile on her face belied that she was much younger than Jack would have guessed originally.

Immediately, she played the upbeat tune of *Bingo*. Most everyone knew the song, and soon several of the patrons and miners began singing the tune as well. In an instant the morose, heavy feeling that had been in the saloon a moment before lightened into something innocent and playful.

"B-I-N-G-O and Bingo was his name-o," Little Natalie sung as well, though still quietly as the song finished. Immediately, the pianist went into a rendition of *Old Macdonald*, much to the little girl's delight.

After a short while, and a few songs later, the children had warmed up enough that Jack felt that they could make it home.

"The sleet seems to have stopped, but the going outside is still treacherous. Let me carry one of the children," Pastor Lamb offered with his palms out to accept one.

"I've had Grace place their wet clothes in a bag and you don't need to worry about bringing the blankets back for as long as you need them," said the barkeep.

Another saloon girl brought a bag, saying, "Here are the children's clothes."

There weren't enough thank you's that Jack could express for how everyone had been so helpful to him. A lump formed in his throat as he said as many thanks as he could to the barkeep, the saloon girls who'd helped, and the many miners who had aided in the search as well. Even in the ice storm. He nodded his thanks to them all as they left.

Ice still lined the streets when they'd made it outside. Pastor Lamb carried little Natalie while Jack had a hold of Nathan. When they made it to the jailhouse, Jack was thankful that the fires in the two stoves were still going, and the living quarters upstairs had warmed. Once upstairs, they both let the children down. The relief he'd felt as both the children ran into the bedroom to greet their grandmother was palatable. He turned to the pastor, having finally come to a determination. "That mail-order bride agency you told me about in Denver, could you let me know how to contact them?"

The grin on the pastor's face widened as he nodded and said, "Immediately."

For another week, Joy barricaded herself in her grandmother's small home, curtains drawn, and doors locked. She jumped at every creak and groan of the old house settling, certain Pomeroy's thugs were coming for her. With no job, no family left, and her reputation in tatters, she felt utterly alone and afraid. Worry and despair overwhelmed her, but she continued to turn to God through bible reading and prayer. Though there were moments where she felt peace, they were not as often as she felt she should have had as a child of God.

Why was going through the shadow of the valley of death so difficult? She knew that God was with her every step of the way. She trusted that His ways were better than hers, and she even found comfort in singing the hymns she knew by heart, but still fear shadowed her and encroached on her constantly. Sometimes she wished that she could just know what God's plan was for her future. But she let out a slow breath as she sat at her grandmother's small dining room table with her bible open in front of her. She knew better than that. It was up to her to live today abiding in Jesus and leave tomorrow up to her Lord.

A stern knock shook the front door. Joy froze, pulse racing. Had they come? Was her time up? She touched the cold barrel of the rifle that she had sitting next to the door. Although she'd been hunting with a friend once and shot a rabbit, could she really shoot a person? Even if it was that villain, Pomeroy or the ruffian he had hired, could she really injure or kill him? She wasn't sure. Holding her breath, she peered through the threadbare curtains. The sheriff stood on her stoop, rifle over his shoulder. Joy's heart sank. There was no hiding, now.

Slowly she unlatched the door, her fingers feeling stiff and achy. Sheriff Hoskins removed his hat, face grim. "Sorry to call on you like this, Miss Stewart, but I've orders to escort you off these premises. You have two hours to collect your things."

Joy's eyes welled with tears. "But Sheriff, this is my home. Where will I go?"

Hoskins shifted uncomfortably. "Can't say, miss. I'm just following instructions. According to the county, this house is owned by Mr. Edgar Pomeroy, and if he says that you're to get out, then I don't have much choice in the matter. You'll have to take it in front of the judge. Two hours now, you hear?" Touching his hat brim, the sheriff descended the steps and waited by his horse.

Swallowing hard, Joy stood on her front porch staring at the man. What good would it do her to take it in front of the judge? Didn't the pastor say that the judges were all in the pocket of Pomeroy and his family? Slowly she turned back into the house, looking around, trying to decide what it is that she should bring. The knickknacks that her grandmother had were things Joy always thought that she would keep, but no, she wouldn't be able to carry them all. So, she chose one, and felt tears sting the backs of her eyes as she held the small bird in her palms and started toward her bedroom and pulled out the steamer trunk. Joy could barely see through her tears as she packed her few belongings. She had no family, and no boarding house would take her if her reputation was ruined. Where would she go? Was she to live on the streets?

Once finished, she pulled her steamer trunk with what belongings she felt she needed outside. Precisely when the two hours ended, the ominous black carriage rolled up, pulled by the two high-stepping dark horses. The door of it swung open and out stepped Edgar Pomeroy, beady eyes glinting. "Well, my dear Miss Stewart, how the virtuous have fallen." He swept off his bowler hat, bowing with mocking flourish.

Joy summoned her courage. "Come to gloat, have you? I've no quarrel with you, sir. Please let me be."

Pomeroy tutted. "Such fire! I admire that in a woman, I do. But you've nowhere to go now, no? Who will hire the disgraced schoolteacher?"

"I'll get by," Joy replied coldly, hoisting her trunk and pulling it down the steps by the handle.

"I think not. Your name's mud in this town,

thanks to my influence. But I am a merciful, generous man. If you take up my offer from before, I'll make sure you have a comfortable place to live and that your reputation could clear up. They still haven't found a new schoolteacher, yet, and I'm sure they could apologize for any misunderstandings about you." Pomeroy stepped closer. "Admit it, you need me, my dear."

Joy turned away from him, knowing the man's offer were nothing but the temptations of the devil. Yes, she was tempted to take his offer, to go back to having a normal life again, but at what cost? She was happy that the trunk had wheels so she could pull it along quicker. "I'll never need the likes of you, sir."

Pomeroy grabbed her arm roughly. "You forget yourself. Your reputation, job, home—all gone at my hand. No boarding house or employer will ever take you now." His nails dug into her skin. "You belong to me."

Joy wrenched away, eyes blazing. "I belong to no one. Not you or any man." And she went to slap him across the face.

His hand flew to catch her by the wrist, and he smiled like a snake about to strike. "Did you think that you'd be able to get away with striking me twice?"

Joy wrenched from his grasp and fled down the road as quickly as she could. The hairs on the back of her neck stood on end.

Pomeroy bellowed after her. "Run, little bunny. Run! There's nothing a wolf likes more than the chase."

Tears coursing down her cheeks, Joy glanced back once to see Pomeroy's beady eyes still aimed upon her, his devilish smile like that of a demon. And the sheriff standing there, powerless. Though ice coursed through her veins, she was determined that she would not be cowed. Chin high, she continued on, praying for deliverance from this evil man's grasp. By God's grace, she would find a way.

Joy hurried along Memphis's dusty streets, casting glances behind for Pomeroy's henchmen. She had to get away somehow. Spotting the church's steeple, she rushed toward it and slipped inside, seeking solace in its quiet calm. Making her way to Pastor North's office, Joy tidied her disheveled appearance, remembering his past kindness. She knocked and heard a voice within call out, "Enter."

At his warm welcome, she pulled in her trunk and sat and recounted her troubles that day with Pomeroy, fighting the sobs that clogged her throat and tears that threatened to overwhelm her. "So now I have nowhere to go."

Pastor North shook his head gravely when she finished. "This is grievous news. But do not lose hope. There is a place where you can go, though it is far away; remember what we discussed before?"

Joy sat straighter, recalling their previous discussion of her grandmother's mail-order bride arrangements. At the time, she had balked at marrying a stranger. But then, she'd still had employment, she'd still had her grandmother's house. But now... "You mentioned the agency my grandmother contacted in Denver," Joy said slowly. "Perhaps it is time those plans came to fruition."

Pastor North nodded. "The morning train could take you to Denver. I will send a telegram to the agency today." He smiled gently. "Sometimes God opens unexpected doors if we find but courage to step through."

Joy decided that sometimes God's plans were fearsome and scary. How could she really leave everything behind and marry an unknown man? But how could she stay when staying was impossible? Steeling herself, she met the pastor's gaze directly. "I will go. Please send word to the agency."

The pastor nodded again and rose to guide her

out of the office. "Let me take you to Mrs. North. I'm certain that we will find a place for you to stay for the night and then you'll be on the first train headed west in the morning."

Pastor North guided Joy through the sanctuary toward the small house at the back of the property where Mrs. North awaited her. Joy's eyes lingered on the festive Thanksgiving decorations adorning the church. Pine wreaths with glossy red bows hung above the pulpit. Stalks of wheat and colorful autumn leaves lined the end of each pew. seeing it all made Joy's heart ache.

The holiday season had always been her favorite time of year. She cherished memories of baking pumpkin pies with her grandmother and hanging stockings above the fireplace in anticipation of Christmas morning. The church was always so beautifully transformed for the holidays, filled with poinsettias, candles, and a towering Christmas tree. Carols would echo from the choir, and Joy would feel at peace.

But this year, as she passed the decorations on her way out, she realized holidays brought only loneliness and uncertainty. Tomorrow morning, she would be boarding a train headed west, leaving behind the only home she'd ever known. There would be no family Thanksgiving meal or reading the Book of Luke through December. How much would change? Joy would be married to a stranger, living in a house that didn't belong to her. But what choice did she have now? She needed to leave Memphis, no matter the time of year.

Yet despite her sorrow, Joy uttered a small prayer of gratitude. Her grandmother had the foresight to make arrangements at the matchmaking agency, providing Joy this slender chance of escape. She whispered thanks that even in death, her grandmother was still caring for her.

As she stepped outside and glanced back at the welcoming lights of the church, she hugged her coat close against the night air. Though her heart remained heavy, she clung to faith that somehow, God would see her through this difficult season. If she'd ever needed a Christmas miracle, it was now.

CHAPTER 5

The train's brakes squealed as it pulled into the Virginia City station. Joy peered out the frosty window at the unfamiliar town that was to be her new home. She had crossed the country by rail with little but a worn carpetbag and her steam trunk. Everything she owned. Now she stepped onto the platform alone, no family to greet her, expecting only a stranger. Despite the brisk December air, Joy took a moment to observe her surroundings. The small depot was decorated sparsely for Christmas. A large pine wreath hung over the entrance and red ribbons adorned the eaves. Down the street, similar wintry embellishments were seen on lamp posts and clapboard buildings. Compared to the grand, glittering trees and lavish displays of Memphis, the decorations here were understated. But they held a simple charm befitting this rugged mining town. Joy wondered what Christmas would be like here, so different from the ones she'd always known.

Even though it had taken three days for her to reach Virginia City from Denver, it had taken just as long from Memphis to Denver. It surprised Joy how small the world seemed to be that she could travel to a whole new world, a whole new town in just a few short days. She'd spent two days in Denver with Madam Willard of the mail-order bride agency there, looking through her options. And she had chosen Mr. Jack Bolling, a Marshall in Virginia City, because he was a lawman, which comforted her, and because he was caring for two small children, twins, who'd lost their mother and father in a tragic accident. The story pulled at her heartstrings. And she'd immediately get to care for and teach young children again, which was appealing for her since she was going to be married and her days as a schoolteacher were left behind her, just as her hometown was.

As Joy made her way toward the baggage car, the wind whipped at her coat and hat. She clutched her worn carpetbag tightly, wary of pickpockets in the crowd, as the men had the look of miners and some of them had taken to staring at her as though she were the only female in town. Her eyes darted about, half expecting one of Pomeroy's men to leap out at her. She feared she may have spotted one—Big Donald—when she was in Denver, but it was a fleeting moment, and she didn't spot him again. Her nerves were still on edge, and she looked around for him everywhere, as though he were the boogeyman, himself.

When a tall figure approached, her breath caught. Was it the ominous enforcer, Big Donald, come to drag her back to Memphis? Though the man was nearly as tall as Big Donald, and close to the right size, there was something different about the way he carried himself. His posture was more gentle, prouder, and dare she think, more honorable. The gentleman neared, and she was met with a kind smile beneath his felt hat, which he removed immediately. "Hello. Miss Stewart?"

She smiled back and nodded toward him. "Yes. I'm Joy Stewart. Since we're betrothed, I suppose you should call me Joy."

Immediately, her face flushed at the thought.

She'd never been called just Joy by any gentleman. She'd never been courted. She'd never been kissed. This whole thing was new to her, and she felt like she'd skipped so many steps on her way to being married.

But somehow, seeing his own cheeks color as he said her name, made her comforted. "Joy, then. I'll ask that you call me Jack as well."

Part of her wanted to deny him, but she knew that would be rude since it was right for them to call each other by name. She gripped the handles of her carpet bag tighter. "All right, Jack."

More heat rushed to her face after saying his name. This was all too much. All too awkward. But what had she expected when she arrived in Virginia City? Her imagination had made it so that perhaps the children would arrive with him. Yes, they could have been a barrier between them, taking away some of the awkwardness. Joy had always been good with children. Adults, not as much. She let out a slow breath, the wind pulling the fog of her breath away. With the heat in her face, she'd nearly forgotten how cold it was there.

"Should I take your bag," the gentleman asked, reaching a hand toward her. "Or do you have additional luggage?"

She pulled her carpet bag closer to herself. "Oh, I do have more luggage. My steamer trunk is right... there," she said as she pointed toward the trunk sitting at the bottom of a stack of baggage from the car. "I'm afraid it seems occupied at this time."

"Not to worry." He huffed a laugh and started toward the baggage men who were still unloading the car. After a few words with them, the boys were smiling and removing the additional pieces of luggage from atop her trunk. Then the strong marshal hefted the trunk and made his way over to her.

"Oh," she said as he drew closer. "No need to lift it. It has wheels."

He blinked at her and then set down the trunk. Then he lifted the handle on the one side and found that it would slide across the wooden platform with ease. "Well, how about that? I didn't even know they made them this way."

"My grandmother purchased it when I was a teenager. She said it was in case I ever got to travel, since she never did and had lived in Memphis her whole life. I was beginning to think that I'd stay there in Memphis my whole life, too and never travel. But I guess she was right, and I was wrong." A knot formed in her throat. Her grandmother had always been right—almost without fail. And at least she'd had the foresight to see that Joy might need a trunk with wheels one day, and even that she would need an escape from Memphis after her grandmother was gone. Joy missed her grandmother's wisdom.

"Well, then. I guess I've got an arm free," he said, jutting an elbow in her direction.

She blinked up at him, unsure what to do. Although she often linked arms with her grandmother as they walked, she'd never done so with a gentleman before. But she knew that it was kind of him to offer his arm to her, so she didn't want to deny him. Slowly, she slipped her arm in and laid her hand upon his forearm. Looking away quickly, she tried to keep him from seeing the color rise to her cheeks as she knew it was there from the warmth.

"I thought I was going to have to rent a cart from the livery man, but it seems that with these here wheels, we could walk down the street just as easy as ride, if you don't mind?"

"I don't mind," she said, her voice sounding small and quiet as it made its way past her tightened throat. She didn't mean to sound coy or shy, even though she was feeling a bit that way. This whole experience was new to her, and she wasn't yet sure how she should feel or behave in this situation. As they made their way across the boardwalks and occasionally stepping down into the dusty dirt of the road, people of all kinds greeted the marshal. They shot interested glances at her, but didn't ask who she was, but rather just nodded greetings her direction as well. It seemed that the marshal was a popular man in town and seemed to know just about everyone.

That comforted her in some small way. Just like the fact that he was a lawman, and honestly, she even found his size to be equal parts intimidating and reassuring. Jack Bolling didn't seem like the kind of man who would be daunted by Mr. Pomeroy and his ilk. Still, it seemed so different here in the mining town of Virginia City than it had been at home. Most of the people they saw along the way were men, and it didn't seem that there were many females her age at all.

She let out a slow breath. Home. Memphis. That wasn't her home anymore. She'd have to get used to calling this place home instead. After walking for a little more than half a mile, they stopped in front of a jailhouse. She blinked up at the building with bars upon the windows and then at her escort.

Rubbing the back of his neck with his free hand after setting down the trunk, Jack looked chagrined. "It isn't much but a small space over the jailhouse. I've been looking for a house that we can stay in together as a family, once we get situated. Then I'll hire a deputy or two to watch over the jailhouse and live upstairs. But for now, this is going to be home."

"Home? Are we to be married right away then?" She took the building in again. It was so different than she'd expected and then another thought occurred to her. Was she expected to live here... with him... without an escort besides the two small children? What if he was rougher than he looked? What if he expected things from her that she was not yet ready to give? She was beginning to feel that this was all a big mistake.

"I didn't mean to frighten you, Joy. And I don't want you to feel pressured in any way. The pastor suggested that we take two weeks to get to know each other before our wedding. If anything that happens here makes you feel uncomfortable or that this whole circumstance isn't right in any way, I don't want you to feel obliged. I will be happy to pay for your ticket back to Denver so that you can find a more suitable match."

She swallowed hard, getting the feeling that this man was every bit as kind as his eyes promised. Then she nodded. "I thank you for the offer, and I will tell you if I change my mind, but I prayed about this and feel that coming here is the right decision. I'm just not sure about the living situation for now. Are you and I..." she paused, more heat rushing to her cheeks. "Are we expected to live together... unwed and alone?"

His eyes widened as she got the gist of what she was asking. "Oh, no." He shook his head. "My mother and the twins will be with us. It's a small two-bedroom apartment, you'll see. My mother and the twins will stay in one room, and you'll take the other. I've already been sleeping in one of the bunks downstairs, since the twins were using the room we've made up for you. But Mother is all right with sharing with them, since she loves them as much as I do."

The way his eyes lit up when he talked about his loved ones assured her even further that this was the right man for her to have chosen. In fact, it seemed that providence had been leading her every step of the way right here to Virginia City. Maybe this was the miracle that she needed. She steeled herself and gave his elbow a gentle squeeze. “I can’t wait to meet them.”

His gentle smile grew to a wide grin. “And they are just as excited to meet you,” he said and then released his elbow from her so that he could open the door. “Let’s head upstairs.”

CHAPTER 6

It had been almost a week since Joy had arrived in Virginia City, and Jack was happy that she was there. He'd been unsure at first, but the twins hadn't been so well behaved or so focused since they'd lost their parents. They had become downright feral before Joy arrived. Jack hadn't really realized how difficult it was to get them dressed and eating meals well, until now that they were doing them almost as well as little adults. He just thought they behaved like children were supposed to behave, but looking back, he realized that neither he nor his mother had any semblance of control or respect from the children. Yet somehow, Joy was able to get them to do whatever she needed them to with her soft voice, smile, and encouragement. They listened to her every time.

If a nanny was what he'd wanted before, he didn't even realize that this could have been the result of a good one. Even now, she had them sitting around the kitchen table when he arrived a little early for dinner. They were threading popcorn and cranberries onto string. He frowned as he approached. "Won't they hurt themselves on the needles?"

Joy looked up at him suddenly with a smile that made his heart patter a little faster. She hadn't seemed to notice him there. "Oh, no! I made them myself so that they are safe for children. I whittle down wood so that it has a large eye and a blunt tip. I call them crafting needles. It also helps children learn to sew using burlap, too." She held up one of the needles in her hand.

Taking it, Jack eyed the oversized needle carefully. It was about four times larger than a regular needle, with a hole that made it easy to thread. He pressed it against his fingertip and nodded and handed it back. "I guess that's not going to stab anyone too easily."

The smile never left her as she shook her head. "Not at all."

Mother's fever had broke only a day or two after the ice storm, but she'd needed rest, so Jack had sent the twins to live with Mrs. Lamb at the church until the day that Joy had arrived. *Joy had arrived*—what an appropriate turn of phrase. For when the apartment they lived in was devoid of the children, it had seemed bleak and lonely and cold. Barely livable. Even though they had wild run of the jailhouse and apartment, and were difficult to control in any way, Jack and his mother were happier with them there then when they were away. He hadn't realized how much he would miss them while they were gone for that week. Once his mother recovered, she asked for them repeatedly, but he still felt it best that she continue to rest and not care for them on her own. They needed help, and Jack was the first to admit it. Now the home felt full and warm and downright Christmasy. Every day since Joy arrived, the house seemed to smell of gingerbread or other cookies. The walls were decorated with crafts she had taught the children how to make. Paper angels and snowflakes and garlands that they had stamped with green and red stars using potatoes—who'd ever heard of such a thing? They'd even made a clothespin nativity scene to set upon the mantle, and she had been crocheting the children stockings with his mother. His mother even looked healthier and happier than he'd seen in years. She had more color to her cheeks.

Joy fed them all well with meals cooked in a timely manner and had the children on a disciplined routine. She amazed him with everything she did. It was as though they received a miracle the day that she came into their lives. And when they were in the home, she seemed calm and assured. But there was something else behind her eyes when they were out and about. He'd noticed that she often looked behind her when they made their way to church or to the general store. She didn't want to take the children out alone, so she'd been getting Mother to go outside with them frequently but not for too long, since no one wanted Mother to stay out in the cold long for her health. Still, it was good that Mother was getting fresh air. Jack watched Joy's confident mannerisms as she cleared the tabletop of the decorations they'd been making, and had the children help her with setting the table afterward.

"Today, Natalie, Nathan and I made sugar cookies. We decorated them and set them in the cupboard rack to cool where little fingers can't get them. Tomorrow, we'll put them all in gift bags and we'd like to give them out to the neighbors down the street. Even if they are local business merchants, we know everyone has families. Do you think we could do that with the children after lunch?" Joy asked, looking up at him expectantly.

He nodded to her as he gripped the back of a chair at the table, thinking on what he had to do tomorrow. "I can go with you, I believe."

Her smile widened as she took hold of a towel to pull the biscuits from the oven. "Excellent."

"Can I help you with those?" He leapt forward, grabbing another towel and took the baking sheet from her. Then he held it in such a way that allowed her to take the biscuits out and place them in the bread basket and cover them with a napkin. He then took the sheet and replaced it in the oven since there was no space for setting it down anywhere.

Once they had everything ready, they all sat down at the table, and Jack said grace over the meal after they all held hands. This was another thing that Joy had implemented, that the children seemed to like. No, it wasn't just the children. Jack had to admit that he also enjoyed holding hands with Natalie and his mother as he said grace. The feeling of their hands united in his made him truly feel like his family was going to be all right, even with the loss of Penelope. For a while there, they had barely been surviving. And even though Joy had only been there for a little less than a week, she was making their house seem like a home and their fragmented family, complete. And if Jack had to admit it, he had feelings of affection and friendship for Joy. She was pretty and had a smile that lit the room. He felt comfortable around her, and she had a way of taking the awkwardness out of any situation when there was silence. Her quiet confidence was reassuring to him as well as the children. Honestly, he couldn't have imagined a better situation with a nanny or another mail-order bride.

During the meal, the children prattled excitedly about the things they had learned that day from Joy, from their letters to numbers to counting and all the basic stuff they wouldn't even be learning until they got to school. Jack had to admit that it was a blessing that Joy was a schoolteacher as well. When they finished the meal, Mother helped Joy clear the table, but before they started on the dishes, they all sat down again, and Mother brought Jack the family bible.

Another of the habit that Joy had implemented was reading to the twins to help them settle down after dinner and before the rest of their routine to get ready for bed. And since it was December, Joy had asked that they continue the tradition that she and her grandmother had of reading the book of Luke. Since there were twenty four chapters in Luke, she said it was perfect for helping the family, especially the children, to remember what the reason for celebrating Christmas was. So, Nathan settled onto Jack's lap and Natalie on Joy's, and even Mother sat down with everyone as he read from the fifth chapter of Luke.

Once he finished, there were yawns and sleepy eyes between the twins, so they carried them off to the bedroom to get ready for bed. Once everyone was settled in, Mother lay with them and the twins were almost asleep before they'd even left the room. Joy was humming a hymn as she headed to the kitchen to clean up.

Jack followed her and came up beside her with a towel. "You wash, and I'll dry?"

She nodded with a smile and started on the first plate.

"I'm really glad that you answered my advertisement. The children enjoy having you here and Mother and I have found it to be a blessing. But is there anything you have need of? Is there anything that we can do to make your life here better?"

With a shrug, she shook her head and handed

him the washed plate. "Everything here feels homey, and every need is taken care of. I hate that I'm displacing you from your bedroom though, so that you're sleeping in a cot downstairs."

It was his turn to shake his head. "Don't trouble yourself. The cot's not too bad, and besides, this is a temporary situation..." He suddenly realized the possible misinterpretation of his words and heat rose to his cheeks. "I mean, with our family growing like it has, we'll need to find a real house for the twins to grow up in. The small apartment above the jailhouse wasn't meant for raising a full family."

"It's not so bad, while the children are little, but I suppose as they grow, it might become a little bit of a tight fit."

"My thoughts exactly." He took the next washed plate from her and dried it with a towel before replacing it in the cupboard. "I know that I speak for all of us, though, that we want for you to be as comfortable as possible, so don't hesitate to ask for anything you might want or need from any of us."

Handing him another plate, she offered a small smile. "I'll keep that in mind."

Jack couldn't help but watch her. This whole thing was much better than he'd ever imagined it would be like to be married. His betrothed was beautiful, and seemed to love Natalie and Nathan as if they were her own. Part of him wished that she could have met Penelope, as his sister would have been great friends with Joy. His heart squeezed in his chest at the loss of that great friendship they could have had. But was he being selfish? It took a great deal of work for Joy to do all that she was doing in their household. She did almost all of the cleaning and cooking and the care of the twins. Mother helped as much as she could, but Jack knew it wasn't even near half as much as what Joy was doing.

And Jack, himself, was busy most of the day with his duties as the only lawman in Virginia City. Though it was a rough town, with miners and drifters looking for work coming and going, it settled down a bunch when the weather turned cold. And the flow of drifters decreased as well, leaving behind the residents of Virginia City who were, in general, a good group of people. Still, he couldn't spend much time in the home helping with the duties of managing it. And his dream still remained of having a house in town, or just outside of it, like he'd had while he was growing up. One that would allow the children to play in a yard and Joy could have charge of without losing that confidence she seemed to when they were in town. He wanted to bring it up, but it didn't seem right in this peaceful moment, when he could just daydream about the peaceful future he could have here with Joy. But maybe these were all dreams he had for himself. Maybe Joy would decide when the time came that she didn't want to marry someone like him, and for some reason, the thought of that sent a prick of hurt through his heart.

THE NEXT DAY AFTER LUNCH, THE MARSHAL KEPT HIS promise to Joy and was ready to take her and the children out for a walk along the street so that they could distribute the Christmas cookies they'd made. Joy was excited to get to go outside for a bit in the weather, and to greet her neighbors. There was a time when she would do this sort of thing often, and when she had no fear in being out in the open. But ever since her grandmother's funeral, fear had eaten at the edges of her consciousness, and it just felt better for her to remain inside. Even as they walked between shops, she couldn't help but look around to see if anyone sinister was following. But within the shops, she felt as though she could draw a breath of relief.

By giving the children specific tasks, she knew that they would stay focused and not often go off to do something on their own. When they were in the general store, she asked them to get the raffia and epsom salts she needed and had the children help bag them and then help to carry the bag with them as much as they could. When they stopped at the seamstress, they delivered their cookies and then looked through the scraps of fabric to find their favorite colors, as Joy bought them with the intent that they would use them to make a calico table runner for Christmas. After giving a bag of cookies to the barber, she had the children help sweep up and dump the trash for the shopkeep. The last stop they made was at the church where they spent a little bit of extra time to allow the children to play with the pastor's children, who although older, were still considered great friends. She let out a contented sigh as she watched the children play. Although she missed her students in Memphis, taking care of the twins had helped fill the emptiness left behind.

And she used everything she could think of to keep the children as busy as possible indoors so that they didn't miss going outside so much. But even now as she watched them run out into the church yard, that same fear of going out with them crept up, and she could feel the tension in her shoulders as she followed them out of the front of the church. Immediately, she looked around to see if there was anyone watching.

"Who are you looking for?" the marshal asked from behind her.

His question came as such a surprise, that she let out a small gasp and her hand fluttered to her chest. She turned toward him and forced a smile, shaking her head. "I'm not looking for anyone."

His brow furrowed a bit, but his eyes remained soft. "Every time you head outside of an establishment, you look both ways almost like you're crossing a street. Occasionally while walking, you cast a glance behind you too. It's like you're checking to see if you're being followed."

Frowning, she chided herself for being so obvious. Or maybe the sheriff was just astute. She let out a slow breath and turned so that she was facing the children and no longer meeting gazes with him. "I... I hadn't yet told you about the reason that I needed to leave Memphis, but I suppose that I should, if we're to be wed."

"Hmm..." he said, encouraging her to go on without interrupting.

Swallowing hard, she continued, afraid what he

might think of her if she revealed all to him, but deciding that whatever it was, it was better to be fully honest with him. "My grandmother passed away, right at the end of October. Apparently, she had a debt—which she paid by giving her debtor our house. But the debt collector made a claim that she owed more money, interest, and it was a great deal more than it should have been. But my grandmother already had the foresight to know that this would happen, so she made arrangements with our pastor, who was the one person she could trust to be on our side instead of his."

When she paused, Jack asked, "This debt collector was a powerful man, then?"

She blinked. He was astute—she nodded. "From what I understand, he has a reputation for making sure that no debt is ever fully repaid, unless it's paid in full at the time of collection. He... he made an offer that could pay my debt, if I were to become..." she shook her head. "If I were to become his mistress," she breathed, wrapping her arms around herself as if to protect herself from the word or situation. "And when I refused, he besmirched my name, got me removed from my position as schoolteacher, and evicted me from my home."

"A scoundrel then," he said in a fierce manner followed by what sounded like a low growl.

Joy blinked up at him to find a stern expression on his face, his eyes becoming harder than she'd ever seen them as he set his jaw. Her heart fluttered at the protectiveness she found there. This wasn't the response she'd expected. Scorn, shame, maybe even incredulousness was her expectation, but instead, she found him offended for her. Her vulnerability brought out a side of him that she hadn't realized before. It made her want to draw closer to him. And the thought of that made heat rush to her cheeks. She shot her glance back toward the children and cleared her throat. "Yes, a scoundrel."

"Well, you are free of him here, then. You are miles away from Memphis and this man has no power or influence here."

Hoping he was right, she nodded, still hugging herself with her arms. Inside, she deeply wanted to believe that what he said was true, but there was something niggling at the back of her mind, that kept her from being completely comfortable. Even now she had the feeling she was being watched, even though she couldn't see anyone who was watching her, and she couldn't shake the feeling that she'd spotted Big Donald back in Denver. Even though she'd almost convinced herself that it had to be someone else, something inside her told her that she wasn't wrong.

"Marshal Bolling!" a young man called out as he ran toward the church yard. "There's a fight in front of the saloon. One of the men's drawn a knife, and he's been drinking, so he might just use it."

Frowning, Jack started toward the gate of the churchyard, but then turned back toward Joy. "I'm sorry. I have to go. I'll ask Pastor Lamb to escort you and the children back home."

She shook her head. "No need. I'll ask him. You go on ahead."

He hesitated, but nodded and gave her a small smile before running off in the direction of town with the young man who'd called upon him. Joy continued to hug herself as she watched him leave. There was a part of her that felt frightened by the marshal being gone—his presence was reassuring. But she knew better. She shouldn't rely upon anyone more than she relied upon God for her safety and to alleviate her fears. No matter what she might be going through in the moment, she needed to trust that God's ways were better than her ways. Letting out a soft breath and watching it fog her vision for a moment, she shot a glance at the children to make sure they were safe and then headed toward the church to ask the pastor if he could escort her and the children home.

Just then, a hulking form ducked into the shadows of the side of the church building, and Joy's heart leapt into her throat. Was this what she'd been afraid of all along? Could it have possibly been Big Donald? Her heart thudded in her chest, speeding up and freezing her in her tracks. Unable to move or think, she just whispered, "Lord, help me."

And that small phrase gave her a modicum of comfort. With it, her joints unlocked, and then she grew angry with herself for being so afraid. She couldn't live her life in fear. Either he was there or it was her mind playing tricks on her. And either way, she needed to face the truth. Hands drawing into fists, she marched over to the side of the church where she'd seen the form disappear into the shadows. Her heart beat against her rib cage as though trying to find a means of escape, but she refused to give into her fear a moment longer. When she reached the side of the church, she peered into the shadowed area, but saw nothing. Frowning, she stepped around the building and looked around in all directions. Nothing. Had she truly imagined it? Shaking her head, she didn't think so. But regardless, her heartbeat slowed and she felt a bit calmer. With her fear subsiding, her anger and bravado did as well.

The laughter of the children drew her attention and grounded her. Her breath continued to cloud around her but was drawn away as the wind picked up. And then gentle flurries began to fall. Snow. That woke her. They needed to get inside, and Joy needed to get dinner started too. She turned on her heel and started back toward the church.

ONCE THEY WERE ALL BACK AT THE JAILHOUSE, THE warmth enveloped them. The twins, still full of energy immediately ran up the stairs, yelling, "Grandma! Grandma!" And wanting to show her the things they'd brought from the store and from the seamstress. Even from down here, Joy and Pastor Lamb could hear the delighted cries of Mrs. Bolling, wowing over the different things the children wanted to show her. Joy turned to thank the pastor and invited him to get some tea or coffee to warm up before leaving.

"No, thank you," the pastor declined her offer with a smile. "I should hurry back before these flurries turn into something that we need worry about."

"Of course," Joy said, "You're right. Travel safely."

"Thank you," he bowed slightly before replacing his hat and stepping back outside, but not before letting in a bit of a draft.

Had Joy gotten used to the warmth of the jailhouse so quickly, or was the temperature dropping fast outside? She wasn't sure, but decided it was best to stoke the fire in the stove and replace a log before heading up the stairs. The pattering of the children upstairs continued, giving Joy a light heart. She hadn't realized how quickly she could become attached to this life. How could a jailhouse become a home so fast? Mrs. Bolling had been a joy to be around, and the love she had for Nathan and Natalie was as plain as day. Both mother and son adored the children as was evident from the way their lives seemed to revolve around them. And that was a good thing. Young children needed confidence that they could make mistakes and learn and grow, and that they still had the love and support of those who took care of them. It was how they grew up to become strong members of society.

After setting in the log and closing the iron door on the wood stove with a poker, she set the tool aside and stood, dusting off her hands. Then the front door barreled open, causing her to jump back in fear. Two hulking men entered, neither of which she recognized. Panic struck her until she realized that they were carrying someone between them—Jack.

A different kind of fear struck her as she rushed toward them. "What happened?"

Two more men entered behind them, bringing in a ruffian who bared his teeth between them. Her hand fluttered to her chest as he met eyes with and glared at her. Frowning, she ignored the villain and turned back to Jack. "Has he been hurt?"

One of the first two men nodded. "I'm sorry, Mrs. Bolling, but when I sent Colton to go get the marshal, I didn't think the man would actually use the knife."

Her eyes went wide, and she removed the hat from Jack's head, only to find him wincing in pain. "Has he been stabbed? Is there a doctor in town?"

Colton, the boy who'd originally called on the marshal from the church was the other man propping Jack up. "Yes, but he's up at the mountain man, Ray Johnson's house. It'll take more than a couple hours for the doctor to get here, so we brought him to you while we sent someone to get him."

She looked him over and saw where his sheepskin jacket was ripped but the blood there wasn't yet evident. His forehead however had a gash on it and his eyes were half-closed. "He was hit over the head, too?" she asked.

The villain that they'd brought in behind Jack cried out, "I didn't do nothing. The stupid marshal just got in the way. If he hadn't jumped toward me, I wouldn't have stabbed him. I didn't stab him on purpose."

"Shut up," one of the other men said as they threw him into the jail cell and closed the iron bar doors with a clang.

"It's his fault. When he got hit in the head, he fell toward me!"

"I said, shut up!"

"Over here," Joy guided the men with Jack toward the bunk area and office. There wasn't much more than a cot and a desk and a chair in the narrow room, but she had the men lay him on the bed. He winced and reached toward his forehead, looking more awake than he had a moment before.

"What's going on down there?" Mrs. Bolling called from up the stairs.

"Everything's under control, Ma'am," one of the men near the jail cell called back. "We arrested a miscreant is all."

"All right," the woman called back. "Where's Joy? Jack?"

"We're both here, Mrs. Bolling," Joy called as Jack took hold of her arm. Sweat beaded on his face as he shook his head and met her eyes with his intense blue ones. She understood what he wanted. "I'll be up in a moment," she called.

He didn't want her to mention the injury yet, and she wouldn't, but if things were serious, they wouldn't have a choice. Regardless, she'd make that decision when the time came. For now, she needed to tend to his injury. She swallowed hard as she undid the clasps on his jacket and exposed his bloody shirt underneath. He winced as she removed the coat, and Colton's father, Mr. Smith, helped Jack remove his shirt as he sat up. Once she saw the damage, she knew what she needed to do. "I'll be right back with soap, water, and other supplies."

The men nodded, and Jack grunted in response, leaning against the wall as he sat upon the cot. As she raced past the men, the man in the jail cell glared at her and spat. Continuing past without hesitation, she raced up the stairs. Mrs. Bolling and the children sat at the table in the kitchen. "What's going on?" the older woman asked with a worried expression.

After drawing in a deep breath, Joy continued to the sink and answered, “Jack’s been injured.”

His mother’s eyes grew wide as she leapt to her feet. “What?”

“He was stabbed, but the blade had to go through his fleece coat and his shirt. It was enough to give him a good gash and he’s lost some blood, but I don’t think it’s very deep.” After pouring water from the kettle to a pan, she grabbed the towel from the kitchen and then her sewing kit. “Do we have any spirits?”

“Neither of us drink the stuff,” Mrs. Bolling answered, shaking her head. “Are you sure he’s going to be all right? Should I help in some way?”

“There are four men downstairs that can help me if I need. I’ll send one of them to get some whiskey or something. Does Jack have another shirt?”

Mrs. Bolling nodded and rushed toward her room. “Of course.”

Then Joy turned toward the children. “When I get back, I’ll need to start getting the stew ready for supper. Can you help your grandmother get the carrots and potatoes washed, peeled, and ready?”

“Do I haveta touch the onion?” little Nathan asked.

"No, of course not," his grandmother answered, returning from the other room with a shirt in hand and huffing a nervous laugh. "I'll get the onions myself."

The little boy cheered, his sister joining in.

Nodding and offering a small nod of encouragement, Joy took the shirt and held firm to the other items as she slowly made her way back down the stairs, hoping not to spill any of the water. As she passed the jail cell, the villain within called out as though taking advantage of her presence, "What's going on? How long do ya plan on keeping me in here anyway? I have rights, you know."

"I told you to keep your mouth shut," one of the men by the jail cell sneered as he spoke through his teeth. "You stabbed the marshal. Whether by accident, as you claim, or not, makes no difference. You'll be staying in there until the marshal lets you go... if he survives."

The last bit sent a shiver down Joy's spine as she continued past. Of course, Jack was going to survive. His injury wasn't that deep, not by what she could see. At least she hoped. She'd not yet done more than a survey of it. When she came back in, she found the marshal standing and saying, "This is all a big deal about nothing. I'm fine now. It's just a scratch."

"Sit back down," she ordered him in her sternest schoolteacher voice. "It's not just a scratch, and it's still bleeding."

The marshal's eyes widened, and the two men with him both stared at her in surprise. But the marshal sat down and that was all that mattered. With a deep breath, she moved forward and gave the damage a better assessment.

CHAPTER 7

Jack sucked in a breath as Joy stuck her finger in the cut and moved it around a bit. The pain, which had dulled some, came back with a bite. "Is that really necessary," he asked. Was she the kind of woman who liked to cause a man pain? He hadn't taken her as one before.

"I need to determine how deep the cut is. It's fine. It didn't make it past the muscle tissue there."

Blinking, he eyed her. "Do you have medical training?"

Slowly she nodded. "I studied both nursing and teaching at the women's college in Memphis. I wanted to keep my options open, and my grandmother supported my education, so I studied hard and did both."

He studied her calm expression as she dipped the towel she brought in the hot water and began cleaning the area around the wound. He grit his teeth, expecting more pain, but the warmth was actually somewhat soothing.

"Could one of you gentlemen please get me some whiskey or other spirits so that I might use it to disinfect the wound?" She used that same stern voice she'd used earlier that had surprised Jack. He'd always taken her as a very gentle woman, but it seemed that she knew how to put people, and not just children, in their place with firm, direct orders. It was a new side of her that he hadn't seen before, and his heart fluttered in response. There was the calm, reassuring side of her that he'd come to know over their past week together, and the happy, encouraging persona she had with the children. Then there was the fearful side of her that Jack had seen in the churchyard earlier; it had brought out the protective side of him. What had surprised him at the time was that his assurance that he was on her side seemed to calm much of her fear. Now he could see that she was a strong woman who could help and protect him if need be. His affection for her grew each moment.

"Would this do?" Steve Compton stepped in and

asked as he produced a metal flask from inside his jacket.

Her eyes sparkled as she took the flask from him and shook it as though measuring the amount it held and smiled. "Perfect."

With that one word, his heart fluttered again. When had his emotions been so tied to this woman and her actions. They'd barely known each other a week, and Jack could already say that his feelings for her were more than they had been with any other woman that he'd ever known. Was it because of their proximity, or the fact that they were already betrothed that he thought this way about her? If they had just been friends and neighbors, would his affection for her have grown so exponentially?

When she poured the whiskey over his wound, he gasped and hissed. The heat and sharp pain were nearly as unbearable as it had been when he was first stabbed. Then she blew on it, and heat rushed to his cheeks. The feeling of her gentle breath against his skin made him nearly forget all the pain he had a moment before.

"That should also numb the area for the next few minutes while I sew it closed," she said quietly and then began threading a needle. This wasn't one of those blunt wooden ones that she'd shown him before. It was smaller, metal, and sharp, as a needle should be.

As she leaned in for her first stitch, he held his breath, but after she pulled it tight and continued, he realized that she was right, the pain was bearable, and other than the pulling and tugging, he'd hardly know she was sticking a needle through his skin. He let out a slow breath as her practiced hands worked diligently. Her brown eyes were focused on the task and her lips were pursed as he watched her. It wasn't longer than a minute or two, but enough for him to heat up again at the thought of her proximity and the touch of her fingers. He cleared his throat and looked away when she bowed her head close enough to kiss his chest and cut the string with her teeth.

"There," she declared, wetting the towel once more and wiping the area. "It's finished. It should heal enough that I can take the stitches out in a little over a week since I didn't have catgut. But don't stretch the area while it's healing. If you pull the skin from the stitches, I'll have to do it all over again and the count to ten days starts over as well, got it?"

He couldn't help but smile at her as that stern voice came back. Nodding, he picked up his shirt to see if he could put it back on, but found it covered in blood. Joy took it from him gingerly and then handed him another one. "I'll clean this one and the jacket."

"You don't have to do that," Jack said. "I'm quite used to doing my own laundry."

She shook her head. "I said not to stretch the area on your stomach. You need to let others help you to make sure you take care of it while you heal, so that means, no laundry,"

He frowned, but nodded so that she knew he understood.

After taking hold of the pot she had and the soiled clothes and towel, she stood and asked, "It will be about an hour before supper is ready, would any of you gentleman be joining us?"

Steve and Gerald both shook their heads and mumbled a negative consensus, and then Joy stepped out into the remainder of the jail house and repeated her question. Colton and Bart both shook their heads and declined, but Robert, in the jail cell sneered. "I wouldn't mind a good hot meal, if you're offering one. As long as you feed me with your own pretty little fingers."

Indignation rose up in Jack and he stepped forward, ready to give Robert a piece of his mind, but then Joy stood up with her spine straight and head held higher. Then she started in with that stern voice, this time with a disapproving air to it. “It might be my duty to feed you as a prisoner here in the jailhouse, sir, but I am not required to cow to your degenerate speech. You’ll find that most ladies do not like being spoken to the way you would a saloon girl, and if you don’t like your meat over salted, it would do you well to show respect to your marshal’s betrothed.”

Robert’s eyes widened behind the bars of his cell, and his jaw went a little slack before he bowed his head slightly and said, “Yes, ma’am.”

Jack couldn’t do much more than stand there blinking at her as she continued up the steps to the house upstairs. What kind of woman was Joy exactly?

“That’s a heck of a woman you saddled up with, there, Jack,” Steve Compton said as he slapped him on the shoulder and came up next to him. “She’ll definitely keep you straight.”

Still watching the stairs even though it had been several seconds since Joy had disappeared, Jack couldn’t help but nod and huff a laugh. She really was something to behold.

"THE WEATHER AROUND HERE FLUCTUATES SO MUCH," said Mrs. Bolling as she stood in the sun, fanning herself as the heat of the day approached. "It's because of the mountain. Sometimes it's colder here than the valley, sometimes warmer. You never can tell."

Joy nodded, feeling a bit overdressed herself. She'd had the idea of helping the children make pinecone fire starters for Jack for Christmas. Useful, handmade gifts were always the best gifts children could give to their parents... or in this case, uncle.

"This one?" Nathan asked, holding up a pinecone.

"That's a pretty one," Joy said with a smile, admiring it. "But it's a little tight for a fire starter. We want the ones that are more open because they work better for starting fires. But we'll keep this one and paint it green to use as a miniature Christmas tree. Does that sound good?"

Nathan nodded and then ran off to join his sister to find more pinecones. Though it was a bit hotter than it had been of late, there was still a cool breeze that went through the pine trees in the copse they stood on the edge of. Joy lost sight of the children for half a moment and then called out to them, "Don't go too far into the woods, children. Stay nearby!"

"All right!" Little Natalie called back, and the two children moved closer to the edge of the woods again.

Joy breathed a small sigh of relief.

"Have you decided yet?" Mrs. Bolling asked as she stood next to Joy.

Blinking, Joy glanced at her. "What's that?"

"It's been two weeks since you arrived. And Jack hadn't yet made firm arrangements for the wedding, but it's been about time for it. It's not entirely right that you just continue living with us, taking care of the children without even getting paid."

The conversation made Joy's chest tighten. She swallowed back against the tightness forming in her throat. "I... I hadn't thought much about it."

That was a lie. The decision of whether or not she should marry Jack weighed heavily upon her constantly. But she kept pushing the thought aside. Getting into a marriage without love had never been something she'd considered before. She loved the children. She enjoyed the life here she had in Virginia City. But did he love Jack? Certainly, she had affection for the marshal. He was kind, generous, protective, and patient. It seemed he was that way with everyone in town, and not just that way with his family. Not just that way with her. She was just another of the current residents of Virginia City. One of its citizens now, right? He didn't seem to treat her differently than anyone else.

What did she expect exactly? Dates and courting? Holding hands and stolen kisses? Heat rose to her cheeks at the thought of that last part. She shook the thought from her head. No. That wasn't what she was expecting. But Jack didn't seem to treat her differently from others. He was the same kind man to everyone that she'd met with him so far. Maybe he didn't have any sort of feelings for her. Maybe he didn't really want to marry her. And why did those kinds of thoughts cause her to feel a bit sad, and make her stomach churn a little in a disappointed way? She let out a slow breath and smiled at the children as they approached her with two more perfect pinecones. "Those are great," she said in a cheery voice as she took them both and put them in the burlap bag they'd brought for the job.

"Well," Mrs. Bolling said. "You'll both have to make up your mind soon. The town already considers you his wife even though you're not yet married. And if you're going to decide to be leaving us, it's best if you do it sooner rather than later. It'll be harder on the children—on everyone if you decide you don't want to stay once everyone's attached."

Joy nodded in understanding. She didn't want to hurt the children—but part of her had no worries there. Likely she was going to find some way to stay nearby, even if Jack decided this marriage wasn't right for him. Maybe she could find work as a schoolteacher or nurse somewhere out this way. Still these thoughts didn't sit well with her. They didn't make her happy, and somehow made her sad. Honestly, she liked her life just as it was and wished that it could stay this way for a while. But she understood what the elder woman was saying, since it wasn't right for things to remain uncertain as they were now. Children, as well as adults, needed predictability, certainty, and routine. Right now, the twins had that, since they had no understanding of how this situation was temporary. How great it was to be so innocent, and to know that everyone around you loved you. But the last thing she wanted to do was to force Jack to marry her if he didn't want to.

Affection. That's what she had for Marshal Jack Bolling. It might not be love, but it could certainly grow into something more. Was that enough reason to get married for now? Swallowing hard, she glanced over toward Mrs. Bolling and saw how sweat was beading on her forehead and running a bit down her temples. Joy frowned. "Are you all right?"

Mrs. Bolling had begun fanning herself. "It is mighty hot."

Glancing back toward the children, she called out, "Bring me one last pinecone, little ones, and that will be enough! Let's go ahead home and get a snack."

"Yay!" the two children called out as they ran over the pine needles and back toward them, each with a pinecone in hand.

Somehow bribing children with a snack always seemed to get them to move just a little bit faster. Joy eyed Mrs. Bolling again. "We should have brought a parasol."

Mrs. Bolling shook her head and waved a hand. "Oh, no. Of course not. I'm fine. But it might be best if we went ahead back inside and out of this sun. I think we've gotten quite enough for the day."

Joy smiled and took each of the children by the hand and started walking with them back toward town and the jailhouse. After they had gone a little ways, Joy picked up Natalie while Mrs. Bolling held Nathan. They walked for a little while that way, until they drew near the general store. Then both children wanted down so they could look in the storefront window. Mr. Miller at the general store made new displays weekly, and as Christmas drew near, there were all sorts of fanciful displays. This week, there was a beautiful nativity scene decorated with bows of tinsel over it and a golden star. Natalie pointed. "It's just like in the story."

Joy nodded, happy that they'd been reading Luke to the children and that the children remembered. After taking a long moment to look at the display, she ushered the children along again, since they were trying to make it back home and allow Mrs. Bolling a chance to rest. They made it most of the way to the jailhouse when Mrs. Bolling said, "Oh, I forgot. We're nearly out of flour. I was so distracted by the nativity display that I forgot that I wanted to pick some up on the way back."

"I'll go get it if you'll get the children home?" Joy offered.

"Oh, thank you so much, dear. I can do that."

With a nod, Joy handed Nathan the burlap bag and asked him to carry it for his grandmother and then told both the children she'd be right back with a pat on the head and turned about, marching away quickly so that she could get back home directly and make the children the snack she'd promised. She supposed if she was late that Mrs. Bolling might do it, but there was no reason for her to be more than ten minutes behind them.

Once inside the general store, she waited behind Mrs. Garner, the wife of the Barber, while she was making her purchase. Mrs. Garner prattled on about how her son was going to be coming home from Boston where he went to school for the holiday and how they were going to be meeting him at the train station tomorrow. When the lady glanced back at Joy while speaking, Joy nodded and smiled. "I'm sure you're all excited."

"Very," Mrs. Garner said with a smile. "You'll have to meet him. Gregory is going to be a doctor."

While the woman preened for a moment, Joy allowed herself to be excited with Mrs. Garner, since the older lady's happiness was infectious. It was funny how so many in town just accepted Joy without introductions and knew who she was on sight. It was warm and welcoming there, and not very much like Memphis at all, where everyone stood on pretense and didn't often greet strangers. When Mrs. Garner was leaving, Joy waved her goodbye and then turned to the counter where Mr. Miller stood with a welcoming smile as well. He asked, "What can I help you with?"

"I need two pounds of flour if I might?" Joy

asked, and then waved toward the window. "The children love the display, by the way."

Mr. Miller opened a barrel and set a paper sack upon the scale, then looked up toward her. "Excellent! I'll let Mrs. Miller know. She's the one who did the display this week."

Joy nodded. "I'll tell her directly when I see her, too."

He scooped in some flour and checked the marker on the scale. "I know she'll appreciate it even more to hear it from you, herself." Once he'd finished weighing it on the scale, he folded the top of the bag over and fastened it and then pushed it across the counter. "I'll put it on the marshal's tab."

"All right," Joy said with a smile as she took the bag. "Thank you."

"Anything else for you?"

She shook her head. "That's all. Have a nice afternoon."

He waved as she headed out the door, the bell overhead jingling as she opened it.

The wind had picked up outside, and the sky had darkened a bit. She glanced up at it and saw that clouds had overtaken the sunshine while she was inside the store. Though it didn't quite look like rain yet, she decided to pick up her pace and strode quickly along the boardwalk, stepping down when she reached then end. After taking her three strides in the dirt, she got ready to hop up onto the step of the next boardwalk, in front of the haberdasher, when a large shadow moved in the alleyway to her right. She caught it with the corner of her eye but didn't have a chance to turn her head. Instead, rough hands grabbed ahold of her, one of them slapping over her mouth just as she inhaled to scream.

CHAPTER 8

Jack was sitting just outside the train station, waiting on the circuit judge to arrive from Carson City when the first drops of rain started to fall. A frown tugged his lip as he peered up at the darkened sky. The Farmer's Almanac didn't say anything about rain today, but these clouds didn't look as if they'd amount to much, and it wasn't cold enough for it to be flurries. The train whistle blew from not too far down the track, and Jack took that moment to duck inside the station. Once the train came to a halt, Jack stepped up to the young gentleman in a suit. He stuck out a hand and offered a wide smile. "Judge Lee, good to see you again. Sorry that you had to come all this way for such a little thing, but the man wants his day in court instead of paying fines outright."

Judge Lee waved the hand that was free of his brown leather satchel and then took Jack's hand to shake. "It's fine. I was heading back to Denver from San Francisco anyway, so it wasn't much for me to stop here."

With a nod, Jack helped the judge get his belongings and escorted him to the hotel in town. He also invited the man to dinner at the jailhouse, proud of his fiancé's cooking skills, but the judge declined saying he'd just get something quickly in the dining room at the hotel. Once it seemed the judge was settled for the night, they said their goodbyes and Jack started to head home. Though the little bit of rain had stopped before it could barely knock down the dust from the street, the wind had continued, taking away the short Indian summer they'd had the last couple days.

The sun was just beginning to set, and Jack was looking forward to getting home. The thought of home warmed his heart. It wasn't just his mother or the obligation and responsibility he had toward the children. The apartment above the jailhouse had become more of a home than it had ever been before, because of Joy. She was making it a home. By her quiet ways and gentle hand, she had brought out the best in the twins like only Penelope ever could before. And the rooms themselves were warmer for Joy's presence. It made it so that he couldn't wait to get home.

Nearly jogging down the boardwalk past the general store, he hopped down the last step and walked across the area by the alleyway. Frowning, he stepped past a small pile of white on the ground and wondered if someone had dropped some of their flour there. He looked around, but didn't see anyone nearby, and since the wind had flattened the pile of flour some, he could assume it had been at least a little while since the flour made its way to the ground. Shrugging, he hopped up onto the next step and strode down the boardwalk in front of the haberdasher and the seamstress. After a couple more boardwalks, he made it to the front of the jailhouse and headed inside.

Immediately, he noticed that the fire in the downstairs wood stove was out. Not entirely unexpected, since it had been a bit warmer that day than normal, but he'd have thought that with the chill in the air outside now, that someone would have started the fire. He set his hat on the coat rack and stepped up to the stove and started putting in the kindling. The iron door creaked on its hinges.

"Jack! Is that you?" Mother called down the stairs a moment before she stomped down them with a worried expression. "Jack!"

He frowned as he threw a match into the stove and stood. "What is it?"

"Did you see Joy in town? She went to the general store just to pick up some flour and hasn't been back. It shouldn't have taken her more than ten minutes, but it's been more than an hour."

"Flour?" He blinked up at his mother, remembering the spot of white that he'd seen in the dirt.

"Yes," she said, wringing her hands. "Why hasn't she returned? Could it be she's decided that this life isn't for her and left? Would she really do that without saying goodbye? All of her things are still here. But what else could have happened to her?"

A few days ago, she'd told him about all her fears in the church yard and how she'd thought that the trouble may have followed her all the way to Denver. Was it possible that the trouble even followed her here? To Virginia City? His heart skipped a beat. Frowning, he looked back up at his mother. "Are Nathan and Natalie here?"

She waved up the stairs. “I gave them a snack and laid them down for a nap.”

“All right,” he said as he grabbed his hat off the coat rack. “Stay here and keep an eye on things. I’ll go look for her.”

“I will. And I’ll pray,” she said, still wringing her hands.

“You do that. We need the Lord’s help more than anything else right now.” He buttoned up his coat and started out the door. The wind had picked up further, and with it, the chill had increased. It felt like a storm might be coming, causing him to frown. He didn’t have much daylight left either, and he feared that he might not be able to find her after dark. What should he do first? Should he start looking on his own or put together a posse? Indecision weighed upon him. If it was as he feared, and there was villainy afoot, he’d be better off with other armed men around to back him up. But what if there was another reason she was missing? What if his mother’s fears were right and this was Joy’s choice. He could respect that on his own, but could he deal with the embarrassment of several people in town being present for his rejection?

Before he could even make a decision, he was at the place where he saw the flour on the ground. The pile was now entirely gone except for a smear of white that was barely noticeable. The wind was already stealing the evidence away. If it had been windier earlier, Jack may not even have noticed the smear of white as flour to start with. He peered down the alley which was now almost completely covered in shadow. Frowning, he stepped into the area with a hand on his pistol. Just behind a barrel, he found the remainder of the flour in a paper bag. This was definitely the right direction. Flurries began to fall around him, dancing in a frenzy on the icy winds. A storm was coming, and he needed to find Joy before it began in earnest. He knelt closer to the ground and noticed scuff marks that indicated a possible struggle, then he found a small set of dragging marks followed by boot prints. They were heading in the direction of the back of town and toward the old abandoned mine shaft. There wouldn't be enough warmth there if this storm grew any more serious. How could this be happening right now? Could a thug from Memphis really be threatening Joy's life and well-being? And for what purpose?

Anger began to rise up in him as he jogged in the direction that the boot treads suggested. "Hold on, Joy," he said as he gritted his teeth. "I'm coming."

THE FRIGID DECEMBER WIND WHIPPED THROUGH THE abandoned mine's entrance, making Joy shiver uncontrollably where she sat bound against the rough wall. It had grown darker and colder since she'd been sitting alone for the past half hour. The coarse ropes chaffed her wrists, but not as much as the fear churning inside at the thought of her captor's return.

That hulking beast Big Donald had seized her with the brute force of a bear trap snapping shut when she'd stepped outside the general store not two hours ago. One gigantic hand had clamped over her mouth while the other encircled her waist like a metal band, providing no escape. She could still feel his hot, rancid breath on the back of her neck as he'd dragged her through the alley, his grip unrelenting.

"Thought you could escape Pomeroy, did you?" he'd snarled in her ear. "I've come to return you to where you belong, Miss Stewart."

Joy had struggled with all her might, but it was useless against the power of the hardened thug. It wasn't far from the edge of town that he dragged her before he knocked her on the side of the head and gagged her and tied her up while she was senseless and dizzy. Then he threw her over his shoulder and carried her the rest of the way. Her screams were muffled, and she beat against his hard back with her fists to no avail. Tiredness had overcome her as she struggled against his restraints. Now, in this decrepit mine filled with decaying tools and tracks, Big Donald had left her and disappeared.

So here she sat, alone and shuddering uncontrollably from both cold and dread. She strained her ears for any hint of Big Donald's return, while mustering the courage to keep praying under her breath. She had to believe Jack would move heaven and earth to find her if she did not return home by dusk. He had promised to keep her safe, and as a lawman, he'd fulfill his duty. Her mouth felt dry from her gag. And her heart sank in her chest.

Could she truly rely upon the marshal like she hoped? He was a good, kind man, and he swore to protect the people of Virginia City. But was she any different from any other citizen in his mind... in his heart? Her own heart squeezed in her chest. She wanted to be special to him. Because he had become special to her. It wasn't just the love of the children or the safety that coming to Virginia City had provided her. Even if Jack wasn't a lawman, even if he couldn't protect her, she'd still feel this way about him. He was a good man. A trustworthy man. And the affection that she had for him was growing stronger. They were friends, but with the promise of something more.

As she feared, the sound of approaching boots crunching on gravel echoed down the shaft. Joy's pulse raced as a hulking figure shadowed the front of the cavern. Big Donald had returned. Then there was a shout and a second shadow appeared. The two shadows collided and a gunshot went off. Who was it? Tears began to stream down her face. What if it was Jack? What if Big Donald had killed him? But the sounds of a struggle continued a moment longer, before they were followed by a heavy thud. A dark figure soon returned and filled the mine entrance, backlit by the setting sun. Joy recoiled in fear as Big Donald lit a lantern and set it on a hook closer to her. His hair was unkempt and his shirt disheveled. Blood dripped from his swollen lip. He snarled at her.

"Nothing but trouble," he said as he spat blood against the wall of the cave. Then he shuffled past and into the darkness behind her.

Fear gripped Joy. What had this man done? Had he hurt Jack? Killed him? She struggled against her bonds and tried to scream Jack's name, but it was unintelligible against the gag that remained in her mouth. Tears continued to fall, and her heart broke in her chest as she mourned her marshal and the life that could have been. Then she heard Jack's voice slice through the shadows like a saber.

"Step into the light, coward!" Jack commanded with rage pulsing through every syllable. He had his hat gripped in one fist as he drew closer to the lantern. Joy's heart soared. He was alive. But her elation was short lived when she saw the blood dripping down his face.

Big Donald lumbered past her, marching like a man ready for a fight, and Jack descended on him in a blur of fists, his fury powering each thunderous blow. Joy had never seen anything so violent and winced as the villain lashed out with the same kind of ferocity and landed a few punches of his own. But the marshal didn't give up and continued his assault until finally, he gained the upper hand. One hard uppercut made the thug fall backwards until his head hit the wall of the cavern and the giant finally crumpled.

Breathing heavily, Jack shoved his misshapen hat back on his head and rushed forward to free Joy from her bonds. He loosed her gag and asked, "Did he hurt you?"

Joy could only shake her head, her mouth was so dry and she didn't trust her voice. He untied her hands and then stepped back from her, offering a hand to help her to her feet. Once she stood, she met eyes with him a moment before collapsing into his strong arms. Jack's sturdy embrace steadied her like an anchor as she broke down weeping.

He rubbed her back gently. "It's all right. Everything is going to be all right."

Although the sobs continued to rack her body a moment longer, she found comfort in Jack's warmth. But he didn't ask a single question, didn't move away from her, only offered her his strong shoulder to cry on as she clung to him. Finally, she was able to get ahold of herself once more and pulled away, swiping at her face. In the lantern light, she could see the bruises and swelling forming upon his face and the blood at his hairline which still trickled down his temple. "You're hurt."

He shook his head. "This isn't so bad. I heal quickly and these don't even hurt."

"But you're bleeding."

He touched the wound on the edge of his hairline. "The bullet just grazed me."

Her eyes went wide. Bullet? Big Donald had nearly shot and killed Jack. Her stomach churned as her heart twisted in her chest. He'd nearly died, and all just because of her. Because he'd tried to save her. It wasn't safety that she was finding in Virginia City. Instead, the trouble had just followed her. She couldn't stay. It was too dangerous. What if he'd been killed? Who would take care of Natalie and Nathan? Who would take care of his mother? It wasn't right for her to remain here and cause them to be in harm's way.

"What's the matter? Why are you looking like that all of a sudden?" he asked, brow furrowed.

She shook her head, looking away. "Nothing."

He took her by the shoulder and pulled her back toward him. "It isn't nothing. You just decided something, and the look in your eyes is telling me that it's something I'm not going to like. So please, just tell me. Don't make decisions on your own. Not now. Not in a situation like this. You're too emotional to decide things right now. If you're thinking about leaving, now is not the time to determine that."

She blinked and looked at him wide-eyed. "How... How did you know?"

He shook his head and continued to hold her arm gently. "You have your heart on your sleeve. It's easy to tell what you're thinking, as your big brown eyes tell the tale."

Swallowing hard, she shook her head. “I can’t stay here. It’s too dangerous. Big Donald spoke of Pomeroy. The man is still obsessed with having me back.” She shuddered at the thought of the evil man’s persistence.

“So you’re going to run?” Jack’s jaw tightened, his eyes flashing like steel. “Running isn’t the answer. You can’t live your life in fear of what the villain might do or when he might come for you. No. I will keep you safe. I will make sure that henchmen like this one,” he said as he shoved Big Donald’s leg with his foot. “Will never bother you again. Instead, they will be arrested and tried in front of a court of law.”

“But the law could never touch Pomeroy in Memphis; how can it be different here?”

“He’s just a man, Joy. No different here than any other villain. He cannot buy this lawman, and I don’t believe he can buy Judge Lee, either. The circuit judge is a former Pinkerton agent and a well-respected, honest gentleman. If Pomeroy sets one foot into Virginia City, he will get what he deserves.”

Joy lifted a hand and touched the wound on his brow. “But you could have died.”

“But I didn’t. I’m a trained lawman, Joy. And I will fight for you. You are my family now, and my… my wife, if you'll have me. And I vow to you, that devil will never lay a hand on you again."

Her heart warmed at his clumsy proposal and his promises. Joy knew that Jack's word was his bond, and that she could rely upon him. But was it right to? She wasn't sure, but she wanted to believe in him. Then she gasped. "Your stitches! Did they open up again? Did you stretch them?"

He touched his side and shook his head. "They smart a little, but they are fine. Not bleeding,"

Instead of standing on pretense, she let herself fall into his arms again. Just a moment longer, that was all that she needed. Everything had overwhelmed her. Silently she prayed, asking God to help her to do the right thing. In her heart, she knew that it was in God's word that she should not run from fear, but to wait upon the Lord and trust in Him instead. But was she in the right place? Did God bring her to Virginia City for her safety or was she just deluding herself?

CHAPTER 9

Jack had asked the judge to stay for a week after the trial of Robert Smalley, the man who'd stabbed him, and Big Donald Cassock, the ruffian who'd kidnapped Joy. Both men were put on a train headed west to serve time at the Nevada State Penitentiary in nearby Carson City. But with Christmas so close at hand, the judge was determined to make it back to Denver to be with his brother and sister-in-law. Jack could understand that and saw the judge off on another train going east the following day.

When leaving the station, he let out a slow breath, watching it gather around his face like smoke. The weather had turned pretty bitter over the last few days, and they'd had just enough snow to cover the ground with a smattering of white in areas that weren't trafficked, but most of the rest of it had turned to mud under hoof and foot during the day and froze solid at night. The governor had brought in fresh gravel from the hills in order to line walkways between the boardwalks in the main part of town just in time to keep them from tracking in mud all over the businesses in Virginia City. But Jack still had to cross the street once in order to make it to the church yard.

The sound of children's laughter and play reached his ears before they even came into view. He caught sight of the twins as they ran from Joseph, Pastor Lamb's eldest son, who was only nine years old. Joy stood watching them, but her gaze shot up to him the moment he came around the corner. He hated that she was always so alert, so aware of the dangers of this world. He wished that she could be ignorant of those things, like she should have been, since she was just a schoolteacher and should never have been through the things she had to go through in Memphis that followed her here to Virginia City. But maybe it was all part of God's plan. Providence had brought her here because of those dangers and things she had to go through. If she had avoided those things, she likely would have stayed a schoolteacher in Memphis and never came out all the way here to become his mail-order bride. And he had to say that he was thankful, immensely grateful, that Joy had answered his advertisement.

"Hello, Marshal Jack!" Young Joseph cried out as he scooped up one of the twins and twirled with Natalie before putting her back down. Enormous laughter and screaming came as a result from the game.

Jack couldn't help but smile wider. "Hello, Joseph. Be easy with her now."

"I know," he answered, grinning back. "Will you be staying for lunch? I think that Miss Joy said that Natalie and Nathan will stay."

"If y'all have room for one more at the table, then I will stay."

"Yay!" The children, all five of them, yelled at once, growing louder as they ran around the church yard in a circle.

Jack shook his head at them and then peered back at Joy, who had paled and whose eyes had widened as she looked back at where Jack had come from. His heart raced in his chest, responding to her fear as he turned around and found three men heading in their direction. Two lumbering thugs stood to both sides of the smaller, more mouse-like man in the middle. The one in the middle was dressed in a three-piece suit and had a bowler hat upon his head. He grinned when he met eyes with Jack, and Jack immediately noticed his bucked front teeth. This had to be the infamous Mr. Edgar Pomeroy that he'd heard so much about. His hand immediately went to his pistol. The two thugs froze where they stood, both reaching for pistols of his own.

Still, Jack stepped forward, a hand out in front of him and he ordered, "Stop right there."

Pomeroy halted, that unsettling grin still plastered across his face. His beady eyes flicked from Jack to Joy cowering behind him.

"My dear girl," Pomeroy purred, ignoring Jack entirely. "How I've missed you."

Jack stepped directly into Pomeroy's line of sight, blocking Joy from view. "You'll address me, not her," he commanded the villain.

Pomeroy's eyes narrowed, the congenial facade fading. "Marshal Bolling, I presume? I've simply come to retrieve what's mine."

"She belongs to no one, least of all you," Jack said, his voice steel. His hand tightened on his pistol grip. The thugs tensed, hands twitching near their holstered weapons.

"Now, now. No need for trouble," Pomeroy said smoothly with a wave of his hand. "I'm certain we can come to an...arrangement."

Jack seethed, kicking himself for not noticing this villain sooner. He'd seen the man come off the train from Denver and his two thugs but hadn't realized who he was. Now he was here to make demands and frighten Joy, and Jack wasn't ready for him. "The only arrangement that we'll make here is you joining your henchman, Big Donald Cossack in the state penitentiary."

The mouse-like man laughed and shook his head. "On what charge, marshal? Anything that Big Donald did was on his own accord. You'll find that his decisions and crimes were his own and you'll not have any evidence to link them to me. Big Donald left Memphis and my employ on the same day, some weeks ago."

"If that is so, then why are you here? There's evidence that Big Donald sent a telegram to Memphis on the day that he kidnapped Joy—for you!"

Pomeroy blinked innocently. "Kidnapped! My word. I had no idea that he was capable of such a crime, much less would commit one. If you read the telegram yourself, you'll just see that Big Donald asked me to meet him here and that he had a present for me. I have no idea what the gift might be."

Jack's jaw tightened as he stood, unconvinced by Pomeroy's lies. "Whatever reason that telegram was sent, it was sent to you immediately after Joy was kidnapped and before Donald Cossack was arrested. That implicates you."

The man scoffed and shrugged. "He could have just as easily sent a telegram to his mother. Receiving a telegram is not a crime. You have no solid proof that I have anything to do with Big Donald's misdeeds." His beady eyes shifted and bored into Joy. "Now, why don't we ask the lady herself? Have I ever laid a hand on you, my dear?"

Before Joy could respond, Jack stepped between them. "That's quite enough. I won't have you intimidating my bride." He put a hand on his holstered pistol. "It's time for you to leave Virginia City. Don't make me use force."

The thugs shifted uneasily, gripping their weapons.

Pomeroy glanced at them, then smiled coldly at Jack. "Very well, Marshal. I can see when I'm not wanted." He tipped his bowler hat. "But this isn't finished. Mark my words."

With that ominous threat hanging in the air, Pomeroy turned on his heel and strode away, lackeys trailing behind. Jack watched them go, keeping Joy tucked safely behind him. He had stalled Pomeroy for now, but he knew the snake would be back. Next time, Jack would be ready for him—with reinforcements. He needed a plan to end this threat to his family once and for all. Letting out a slow breath, Jack's grip on his gun lightened. But how? How was he going to arrest a man as slick as Edgar Pomeroy?

JOY DECIDED THAT SHE COULDN'T LET EDGAR Pomeroy make her live in fear, not again. She wouldn't barricade herself inside the house this time and cause the children to suffer because they couldn't get outside and get the sunshine that they needed. No. The last thing she needed to do was allow the children to suffer in any way because there was a villain who was stalking her. So, she determined to go about life and not make her decisions based upon fear. The Lord was her strength and her shield, and as long as she remained in Him, she would fear no evil, because God was with her.

The twins wanted to join the Lamb children in

caroling on the streets on the evening of December sixteenth. Joy had been hoping that the marshal might be able to come with them, but he was riding out to meet the stagecoach that was coming in from Carson City that evening instead. So, it would just be the children, the Lambs, Mrs. Bolling, and herself along with a few other ladies from the choir who would join with their children, totaling twelve little ones and eight adults, but only one gentleman—Pastor Lamb. Though it wasn't the most ideal situation for safety, Joy decided that she needed to move forward and rely upon the Lord for her protection.

The children were singing *Angels We Have Heard on High,* though the twins participated in little more than the "Gloria" part. The songs they sang as they walked along the busy Main Street, decorated in tinsel and holly, made everything feel right with the world. The smattering of snow in drifts along the side of the road and walkways and the nip of chill in the air as dusk drew near reminded them of the time of year. Joy always loved the winter in December, but hated it in January and February. While winter was new and cooling them off from the heat of the summer months, and with the holidays as well, December was one of her favorite months of the year. And this year was even more special because she had a family—a real one, a large one, and she didn't have that lonely longing for more that she'd had even as a child when it was just her and Grandmother.

They continued down the side of the street and were passing the general store when the shop owner came out and passed out Doscher's candy canes to each of the children. As they passed the barber, two of the patrons came out to sing *Joy to the World* with the children in perfect harmony. Then they reached the hotel, and the inn keeper came out to give each of them little cups of hot chocolate. The whole town felt as though they were getting in the holiday spirit, just from the songs of the children.

"Lovely. Lovely," a voice said that stiffened Joy's spine and made the hairs on the back of her neck stand up. "Just lovely. What a wonderful job, children."

Edgar Pomeroy clapped his hands as he stepped out of the hotel in a fur-collared coat with a cigar on his lip. And then he started passing out silver coins to the children. It disgusted Joy and she wanted to jump forward and put a stop to this display, but didn't know if she should. It would scare the children if she did as she felt, and she didn't want to take away from the spirit of giving that they'd been enjoying during their trip through the town. All she could think to do was to usher the children along.

So, she did. She pushed them forward with her hands and body, asking, "All right, children. What should we sing next?"

Luckily the children started moving along, and the next song was *Deck the Halls*, which was one of the twins' favorites since they could sing the Fa-la-la-la-la part to their hearts' content. But as she went to follow the carolers, a hand took hold of her elbow and pulled her back roughly.

"Hold on a moment, missy," the snake's slithering tongue spat in a hiss, too close to her ear. "Why don't you stay a while and let the reverend and his ilk take care of the marshal's children?"

She frowned and ripped her elbow from his grip. "Unhand me, sir!"

He gave a humorless laugh and stepped back, looking around at the other patrons from the hotel as well as the innkeeper who'd been standing nearby at the time. He softened his tone and almost sounded contrite. "No need to make a scene, now. I was just asking for you to give me a little company on this cold night."

"Never," she said vehemently, her hands forming into fists at her sides, and her face heating in her anger. "I would never give you anything you ask of me. Not company. Not attention. I do not wish to spare you a single moment of my time. Not a single thought. I only wish that you would leave me alone!"

Blinking at her, Pomeroy actually had the gall to look surprised and even a little hurt by her response. Then he pulled himself out of it and put on that greasy smile once more and shook his head, donning his mask of bravado. "Surely you're just angry at me still for suggesting that I make you my mistress. Well, you're right. I should never have disrespected you in such a way."

This time it was Joy's turn to blink in surprise. Was he actually apologizing to her?

He stepped forward and leaned in toward her, causing her to lean back in response. Then he whispered, "I should have made you my wife from the beginning."

Ice filled her veins at the sound of his words, and she shivered and took a step back in response. The determination in his voice and the strength of his words had caused her to shudder. A profound feeling of truth came from the meaning of them and she was certain, right down to her core that he meant what he said and believed he had the power to make it happen. No, this wasn't the time for her to believe the devil's lies. It wasn't the time for her to shrink back in fear. If she ran from him now, she would never be able to stop running, and then he would know the power that his words had over her.

Stepping forward closer to him, she leaned in and hissed under her breath, putting as much truth into her words as she'd felt he'd had in his. "You sniveling little snake. I wouldn't marry you if you forced me to at gunpoint."

Then she stepped back and glared at him with as much hatred as she could muster, pinning him with a schoolteacher's scowl. For a moment, his bravado faltered and his smile slipped from his face. She'd affected him, and that made her feel stronger. And with that strength, she turned on her heel and walked nonchalantly back to the children and carolers, who thankfully hadn't seemed to notice her missing.

CHAPTER 10

Since it would be a few days until the next train from Carson City arrived in Virginia City, Jack had petitioned the mayor to hire a stagecoach to make the twenty-some mile route there and back in a day, with a change of teams once they reached the bigger city a little before noontime. Luckily, the mayor of Virginia City had agreed that it was high-time to do some deputizing and to increase the law enforcement in the city. Honestly, it should have happened long ago, since the population of the town, though mostly miners, was reaching well into the thousands, but Jack, being the kind who tried his hardest, had been willing to shoulder the burden alone for too long. So, they sent a telegram to the U.S. Marshal office in Carson City, and also to Judge

Lee, former Pinkerton Agent in Denver, to see if the Pinkerton Agency there could also spare an agent or two at least temporarily.

Although Pomeroy had only brought two thugs with him from back east, he'd been throwing money around in Virginia City, hiring some of the off-color miners and transients and making somewhat of a crew. When Jack brought his concerns to the mayor, there wasn't much else to do but hire on more lawmen. The marshals' office was sending three new marshals to Virginia City on temporary loan, young men without families who would not be missed for the holiday. And Judge Lee had sent a telegram saying they could spare two agents but possibly more after the new year. Jack really hoped that whatever situation was brewing wouldn't wait that long before coming to a head. Especially since he and Joy had decided that they wouldn't wed until after the situation was taken care of.

But it seemed like for every one lawman Jack could manage to hire, Pomeroy could hire two or three new thugs. Over the last few days, Jack had managed to deputize three men, one of which was Ray Johnson, who was more than happy to be back on his feet again and offered up his home to use as a bunkhouse for the deputies until a more suitable place could be found. Jack's search for a home for his family became all that much more pressing of a dilemma, so that the upstairs area could become the bunkhouse for unwed lawmen like it was always intended to be.

Jack kept Red, his chestnut gelding, at a steady jog just behind and to the side of the stagecoach as they continued on toward Virginia City. It was only a mile or two out now, and he could see the lantern-lit streets from top of the hill. He had to hold Red back from loping as soon as the gelding smelled home. Reaching forward, he pat the horse on the neck. "You'll get your oats soon enough, and maybe even a warm bran mash if I can talk Clyde into it."

The gelding shook his head in response, a little bit of steam rising off the melted snow upon his neck. Though there hadn't been much more than flurries, it had been coming down pretty steadily for the last couple hours. When they entered town, he could hear the singing of carolers and children in the distance, and it brought a smile to his face. Christmas was a little more than a week away, and he wanted to make sure it was the best possible time for his family. He just needed to get rid of one thorn in his side, and then perhaps he'd get the best gift of all, a wife who he adored and wanted to protect. But after speaking to the Virginia City prosecutor, he found that he couldn't create a case against Pomeroy without more evidence.

Letting out a huff, Jack dismounted his horse just in front of the livery. The marshals on the stagecoach got down soon after and Jack helped Clyde and the driver of the coach take care of all of the horses before showing the men to the saloon-inn where they'd be staying. The young men couldn't help but smile at the thought that they'd be staying at the inn above a saloon, but Jack hoped that they wouldn't let the wild oats sow too hard, since they were here to do a job, and he needed them to stay serious.

Once they reached the saloon, Jack led them inside and stepped up to the front desk in the foyer before the bar area. "I'm here to sign in my men."

The owner and man behind the desk, Bart Thompson, nodded and turned around his book. "Sign here, and we'll bill the mayor."

Jack signed the guest book and then turned to the three marshals. "These accommodations were the ones that the mayor was able to afford on a weekly basis. Please don't disparage them or get too wild. You'll be bunking in pairs in the two rooms, and I expect you to be bright-eyed and bushy tailed in the morning. Understood?"

The foursome nodded and gave a general, positive consensus, but their eyes were already wondering toward the bar and the saloon girls who were up on the stage wearing green and red sparkling in tinsel, and dancing to *Jingle Bells*. Why did these marshals have to be so young? Jack knew he wouldn't be able to stop them from drinking entirely, so he needed to formulate a plan.

"If you must do any drinking, limit yourselves to two drinks. In fact, raise your hand if you'd like me to pay for your two drinks on the solemn promise that you'll have no more than two."

That got their attention. All three of them pulled their gazes from the saloon area and raised their hands and hooted and hollered like they were ready to start the party.

"All right," Jack said as he entered the bar and walked up to the bartender. He offered the barkeep a bill and said, "I'm paying for these three gentlemen's drinks tonight. They'll get two each and no more, even if they offer to pay for it themselves or if someone else does. Understood? Two only," Jack reiterated, holding up his fingers.

The bartender, Oliver, nodded. "Yes, sir." Then he turned toward the foursome and asked, "What'll you have?"

As Jack started away, he shook his head. He knew that not everyone could be as vigilant about staying sober as he was and how he'd been raised, but he really hoped that these young bucks would stay the course and be worth the help in the long run. He stepped back out into the cold and pulled up his fleece coat's collar. His fingers ran over the stitches that Joy had put in his jacket from where he'd been stabbed. She'd used a tan thread that almost matched entirely with the buck color of the suede on the outside of his jacket. His hat kept the light snow from falling into his eyes.

One of the deputies on duty passed him and tipped a hat to him. That was good. At least someone was on the job keeping peace in the town. Jack couldn't help but feel like something was brewing. The holiday was bearing down on them, and the winter would only get harsher after. If something was going to happen, it was likely to happen before the holiday rather than the dead of winter. Winters in Virginia City could be harrowing because of their elevation. And nights could be especially brutal. He stood under a lamppost decorated with a bough of holly and looked up at it. This time of year was always still bright and hopeful, even though they were heading toward the hardest of months. Faintly, in the distance, he could still hear the carolers, and remembered that Joy, his mother, and the twins were likely out with them singing. Letting out a breath, he decided it would be best to beat them home and make sure the fires were well stoked for when they got back. Maybe he'd even put a kettle on.

WHEN JOY RETURNED WITH THE CHILDREN, SHE WAS happy to find a warm jailhouse waiting for her. Voices carried from the marshal's office in the back, leading her to believe that one or more of the deputies were in there. Then she heard Jack's deep voice, and it rang a note in her core. His voice meant something to her—safety, comfort, happiness. Even though it had only been a few weeks that they'd been together, Jack had proven himself to be one that she could rely upon, and they'd drawn close enough that she was beginning to understand that the feelings of affection that she'd had for him were growing into something more.

The twins were still wild from their night singing in the cold. Gifts that they'd received were stuffed in their pockets to the point of overflow. After they could fit nothing more into them, they gave the excess to Joy for carrying. Candy and apples and the dreaded silver coin were all there. She didn't like seeing the money, but she wasn't going to take it away from the children just because she held a grudge against the gift giver. Letting out a small sigh, she smiled when she saw Jack approaching. The twins saw him first and ran into his open arms. "Uncle Jack! We had so much fun!" Little Natalie cried as he swung her up and held her against his side, filling both his arms.

"I'm happy to hear it," he said, his hazel eyes twinkling as he met gazes with Joy.

Her heart skipped a beat in her chest. Maybe he was just a good man. Maybe he was the protector of Virginia City and treated its citizens with great care. But it didn't matter. He looked at her differently than he looked at everyone else. She could tell that now. Maybe what he had for her was growing into more than affection as well. What she felt when his eyes met her's made her a believer. And she thanked God for bringing them together.

"Dinner will be ready shortly," Joy said as she took Natalie from him, since he held both children. "I've already got the biscuit dough set to rise in the larder, and I'll take it out and bake it, and we'll be ready. Will both deputies be staying for dinner?"

"All three actually. Ray is in town to pick up the other two for the night, so I invited him to eat with us as well."

"You didn't bring the marshals from Carson City with you though?"

"They're at the saloon. They're awfully young, so I think they prefer what the saloon can offer them instead of us old fogeys and children," he said with a laugh.

Joy huffed a laugh with him and nodded. "All right. Mrs. Bolling and I will have supper on the table in twenty minutes or so."

"I really wish you'd call me Mother now," Mrs. Bolling said gruffly. "You're the one who's soon to be Mrs. Bolling."

Heat rushed to Joy's cheeks at the thought, and when she peered up at Jack, she saw that his cheeks had tinged pink as well. Suddenly it became difficult for them to meet gazes with each other, and Joy felt it best to flee from this awkwardness. She started toward the stairs. "I'll call you when supper's ready."

"All right," he called after her, and handed Nathan to Mrs. Bolling as well.

It wasn't too long before they'd finished making their dinner. They'd left a stew on to simmer in the Dutch oven while they were caroling, and found a kettle ready on the stovetop when they came into the kitchen. It was perfect for mixing with milk and honey to warm the children up a bit while she made their plates. They tucked in before the biscuits were finished baking, so they ended up splitting one biscuit between them to clean their plates with. Then she and Mrs. Bolling got the twins ready for bed while setting the table and readying it for the marshal and his deputies. There was only enough room at the table for six to sit comfortably, so she'd made sure the twins were fed and read the chapter of Luke to them to send them off to sleep before calling the lawmen up for dinner.

Once the four men sat at the table, the six of them held hands to say grace. Joy's small hand in Jack's warm large one grounded her and in her other, she held Mrs. Bolling's. This was one of the largest groups of people that Joy had ever cooked for or had dinner with at the same time. It had always just been her and her grandmother. She sent up her own silent prayer of thanks just as Jack said, "Amen."

Then they all tucked in. Metal spoons clanged against the dishes, and there was some small mumble of conversation that was mostly muted by food. The men's mouths were too full while enjoying their dinners. There was a sense of pride that came over Joy in the way that they all seemed to like what they were eating, and she finally realized now what her grandmother meant when she was little and the elder woman would say that just watching Joy eat made her feel full. There was that sense of fullness in Joy now.

"Marshal!" A voice shouted from downstairs, and everyone froze in their eating, mid-chew.

Joy cast a glance toward Jack who frowned, set down his spoon and pushed back his chair as he stood. He called out, "Coming," as he started for the stairs.

The three deputy marshals at the table put down their spoons and followed, with Ray taking one last gulp of his water, nodding toward Joy and saying, "Thank you for the dinner, ma'am."

She nodded back, slowly standing, herself. Mrs. Bolling stood with her. Joy wrung her hands, for a moment, but when Mrs. Bolling set a hand on her shoulder, she looked toward the older woman. Then she nodded and decided that she couldn't just sit here. Joy needed to do something, so she followed after the men and headed for the stairs.

CHAPTER 11

"I'm sorry to bother you at dinner time, Marshal," the young marshal, whose name was Joe said, his hat in his hands. He stood with the other two marshals who were both red-faced from their inebriation. Joe, however, looked fairly sober. "We overheard some of the men in the Cactus Saloon talking about how there was a man throwing around money in the Silver Spur Saloon, so we decided to check out what they were talking about. We followed them to the Silver Spur and caught sight of the man you'd described to us—the easterner with the bowler hat. He'd had quite a lot to drink and was hiring men left and right and inciting them to come with him. It's quite a crowd now, and it seems that they're heading this direction."

Jack blinked. “They’re heading this way?”

“Yessir,” one of the other young marshals said.

Frowning, Jack nodded and then stepped over to the gun rack and began passing out rifles. When he handed one to a marshal who’d been drinking, he said, “It looks like you’ve had more than two drinks, son.”

The boy at least had the fortitude to look chagrined. “Yes, sir. Joe doesn’t drink so Mack and I split his two. Each of us have actually had three.”

Frowning, Jack shook his head. “I’m going to hand the two of you rifles, but they will not be loaded, understood. I don’t want either of you firing off a round and starting something that shouldn’t be started.” He looked up when he heard Joy reach the stair landing. “Joy, could you get these boys a coffee? They need to sober up quick.”

She nodded and raced back up the stairs.

“If there’s a real fight, you boys will have your pistols, but for now, I need you to at least look the part of a lawman with a rifle. It will be more intimidating.”

“Yessir,” they both said together just as Joy came walking back down the steps with a tray of coffees.

“Your mother must have thought ahead and had

a few cups already made. Do any of the rest of you want any?"

"Thank you," said Ray as he and one of the other deputies reached over and took a coffee from Joy.

Seven men. That's all they had to subdue the crowd that was coming. Even though Jack had requested a few Pinkerton Agents, they wouldn't be arriving from Denver until morning. Would seven men be enough to overcome the people who were coming? His heart squeezed in his chest as his stomach flipped and fear wanted to overcome him.

"Perfect love casts out all fear," he whispered under his breath, remembering the Bible verse from First John. Jack drew in a deep breath as he loaded his rifle. No one loved this town more than him. He grew up here in Virginia City. Even though the mines had taken his father's life with the miners' sickness, he loved the miners and the people who ran this town. The scripture gave him comfort. "If God is for us, who can be against us?" This time, he said the Bible verse a little louder, quoting Paul's letter to the Romans. In this situation, he was, without question, on the right side, and he needed to remember that God would be on his side, as well.

"Amen," said Ray, who just finished loading his rifle and set it upon his shoulder.

"Amen," said the other deputies and marshals.

Jack could see the sliver of fear in all their eyes, but he knew that being a lawman took courage, and each of these men had it in spades. He nodded to them and then the each strode outside.

Horror struck Jack the moment he stepped out as he smelled the smoke and saw that a building down the street in flames. He sucked in a breath and jogged out into the street, hoping to get some men called out to start a bucket brigade. But then he noticed the crowd approaching him. Edgar Pomeroy walked at the front of the crowd, a saloon girl on each arm, and he was carrying a pistol that he then shot into the air with a laugh.

The crowd around him numbered well into the thirties or more, each man holding a blunt object or pickaxe. Thirty or forty men...against seven. When Jack looked at the numbers, that fear started creeping back up his spine again. He took a deep breath and pushed it back down. Then he shouted, "Stop where you are and drop your weapons. None of us want to fight today."

"You're not stopping anyone, marshal. Not with that small lot of men behind you. Pomeroy continued to swagger down the street, emboldened by liquor and the mob at his back. His beady eyes fixed on Jack with malevolent purpose.

A frown tugged at Jack's lip. "What's wrong with you, man? Get ahold of yourself. I wouldn't have expected a smooth man like you to behave in this way."

"Ha!" Pomeroy gave a mirthless laugh. "Why don't you ask that woman of yours? What is wrong with her anyway?" He pulled in a saloon girl closer to his side and she giggled in response, wrapping her arms around his neck. "Doesn't that woman know what she's missing? I'm desirable and I'm a man of great means." His beady eyes swirled with inebriation as he turned his gaze back to the saloon girl. "You'd marry me, wouldn't you, Missy?"

"Of course," the girl said as she planted a kiss on his cheek.

That action only made the man sneer and push the woman away. She fell backwards on her hind end, looking up in shock at Pomeroy. But the man only laughed and said, "I wouldn't want a woman like you anyway. Harlot!"

The other saloon girl left Pomeroy's side to help the one who'd fallen. As the crowd pressed around them, the two girls scampered away. Pomeroy fired his pistol skyward again, his men jeering. Jack's hand tightened on his rifle but he held back, not wanting to ignite the powderkeg. None of this seemed like the kind of man Pomeroy was. From what Jack had ascertained, Pomeroy was the kind of man who sent others out to do his dirty work while he stood back. But this time, he was at the front of the crowd. Had Joy's rejection of Pomeroy had this strong of an impact on him? What did the man hope to accomplish?

"I'd advise you and your men disperse peacefully," Jack warned, raising his rifle in one hand to the side and his empty hand up in a gesture of surrender, hoping that the men in the crowd might do the same. "No one wants things to get out of hand."

Pomeroy barked a laugh. "Oh, I think they already have, marshal!" He turned to the crowd. "What say you boys? Should we show this here lawman how we deal with his ilk?"

The mob roared in unison, surging forward. Jack and his vastly outnumbered lawmen braced themselves. Pomeroy climbed up onto a cart to the side and urged the crowd onwards past him. Now that seemed more like the man's mode of operation, Jack thought as he steadied his rifle and yelled out to the crowd. "Stop what you're doing at once! Desist!"

But no one seemed to listen. Jack's only consolation was that these were miners and drunks, none of them seemed to be armed with more than pickaxes and clubs fashioned from chair legs, it seemed. He didn't want to shoot anyone, but if they continued to press forward, he wouldn't have a choice. Just as the two sides were about to collide, a gunshot rang out. Pomeroy collapsed, howling and grasping his leg. All of the crowd froze where they stood, all eyes were on Pomeroy as he writhed in the cart, holding the wound on his thigh. Blood oozed past his fingers. Jack wasn't sure who took the shot, but was glad that it seemed to sober up the crowd immediately.

"Do you want the next shot to hit you?" he shouted his question, training his rifle at the people who stood at the front of the mob. "Drop your weapons! If you comply now, I won't press charges against anyone in Virginia City who took part today so long as you join in a bucket brigade to put out the fire y'all started. I'll speak to the mayor myself."

Sullenly, the men looked around and after the first man threw down his chair leg, others followed suit. Soon, there was a pile of fashioned clubs and mining tools sitting between Jack's lawmen and the crowd, which had dispersed entirely and had moved toward helping with the fire at the saloon.

No men stayed, not even the thugs who'd come with Pomeroy to start with.

Jack approached the cart where continued cries of pain abounded. He peered in the cart at the man who lay there bleeding. Pomeroy's beady eyes still had fire within them as he writhed around, cursing Jack through gritted teeth even though his drunken courage seemed expired.

Marshal Jack Bolling nodded toward his men, drawing them closer as he declared to the man in the wagon, "You're under arrest for inciting violence and destruction of property."

And with those words, a sense of relief came over Jack so hard, that his knees nearly buckled. He glanced down the street and saw that the crowd had already succeeded in dousing the flames so that the bright light of the fire that direction had already been quieted—chances were the bucket brigade had started even before the crowd had dispersed. The danger was over before it had really gotten started. He sent up a prayer of thanks for that. Ray Johnson and another of his deputies, Colton, helped Pomeroy out of the cart and put handcuffs on him.

Jack shook his head and then he eyed his deputies and the marshals. "Who took that shot?"

The men looked at each other with questioning

glances, but none of them seemed to know who did it. Jack frowned. Then he opened his mouth to admonish them so that one of them would come clean, when a small voice called out from behind them.

"I did it," said Joy, who stood behind the men, holding the rifle that his mother kept in the upstairs gun rack on her shoulder. "I'm sorry if I shouldn't have."

Huffing a laugh, Jack couldn't do more than shake his head. He hadn't realized that he'd had eight on his side rather than seven, but that one extra had made all the difference. "No, it's fine. It helped more than you might even know."

Her cheeks tinged pink, and she shyly shook her head. And the lawmen around them started laughing

Ray Johnson laughed so hard, he slapped his knee. And then, wiping a tear from his eye, he said, "It looks to me, that you shoulda been deputizing your future wife, Marshal Bolling."

And that sent the men into even more laughter, causing Joy's face to redden further as she looked down. Jack stepped toward her and scooped her into his arms. "No, Joy. Don't be embarrassed. The men are right. I shoulda deputized you."

Her eyes met his, sparkling in the lantern light. "I was only trying to help."

"That you did, Joy. You did," he said, and caught up in the moment, he leaned in and brushed his lips against hers in a gentle kiss.

Her eyes widened and she gasped.

But when Jack went to pull away, he found that he couldn't. Her hands still gripped his suede jacket. She peered up at him through her eyelashes and then looked back down again. "That was my first kiss."

This time it was Jack's turn to redden. He didn't tell her, but it was his first real kiss, too. Not sure what else he should do, but feeling a little guilty about stealing the kiss, he apologized. "I'm sorry."

Shaking her head, she looked back up at him, the smallest of smiles tugging her lip. "Do it again, please."

A chuckle bubbled up from him as he leaned in and said, "I'm happy to oblige."

Then he lifted her chin with his fingers lightly and stroked her cheek with his thumb. And this time he pressed his lips against hers, and she gripped him tightly, her hands moving to his back. Jack pulled her closer, deepening the kiss.

Until someone behind him cleared their throat,

causing them to both break away from each other. Then Mother said from the doorway of the jailhouse. "Perhaps the two of you should wait for all that until after the wedding. With this mess over, there's gonna finally be a wedding now, right?"

Jack met eyes with Joy, and both of them smiled. Then Joy nodded, and Jack's heart filled with affection for her. He loved her, he could admit that to himself now. And he couldn't wait to be married to her. "Tomorrow if the pastor has the time."

Joy laughed and nodded. "Tomorrow."

"About time," Mother said, as she started marching away, pulling her coat around herself.

Surprised, Jack called after her, "Where are you going?"

Mother waved a hand behind herself and said over her shoulder, "I'm going to see if Pastor Lamb has time tomorrow. There's no use waiting any longer."

There wasn't much else Jack could do other than shake his head. Then he met eyes with Joy, who laughed again. And Jack had the urge to pull her back into his arms and finish what he'd started, but he gripped his rifle with one hand and made a fist with the other. It needed to wait. Tomorrow.

EPILOGUE

Christmas Eve, Jack came in just before noontime for dinner, but Pastor Lamb was with him, and it took Joy by surprise. "Oh!" She said, "I wasn't expecting company. Let me set another place."

Jack shook his head. "Actually, no. We're going to need to have lunch a little late today. Could you pack it up and take it with us?"

Furrowing her brow, Joy tilted her head but started doing as he said, and finding Mrs. Bolling already bringing over a picnic basket. "All right. What are we doing?"

Already, Jack was helping little Natalie with putting her jacket on. Pastor Lamb was also helping Nathan get his jacket, with a big grin on his face.

Somehow it seemed that everyone knew more about what was going on than she did. Peering back up at her, Jack said, "We're going for a little ride to just outside of town."

"A ride?" she asked, feeling even more confused, but pulling on her own coat, nonetheless.

Once everyone was finished, the group, led by Pastor Lamb, headed past the two deputies in the jailhouse below. Joy nodded to them as they passed, and Ray called out, "Merry Christmas."

"Merry Christmas," she responded and then followed everyone out the door as the other deputy said the same. The marshals that had come from Carter City had already returned, escorting Pomeroy by train to the state penitentiary for his crimes. Luckily for Joy, Judge Lee, himself had come as one of the Pinkerton Agents on the train from Denver the day following the riot in Virginia City. He was able to attend the wedding, and then preside over the city's case against Edgar Pomeroy a few days later. Pomeroy had tried to bring up the debt owed to him by Joy's grandmother, but the court had found that it was null and void because the interest was exorbitant, and the judge refused to acknowledge Pomeroy's illegal claims.

As the cart headed to the east of town and

beyond the city limits, Joy's curiosity got the better of her. "Where on earth are we going?"

Jack let out a soft sigh and smiled toward her. "We have a full family now, and as such, we need a home. A real home. The one that I grew up in was given to my sister and her husband when they married and had little Nathan and Natalie. My mother then moved in with me at the jailhouse to give their family peace and space to grow. But then a fire burned down the house unfortunately with Penelope and her husband within," he paused and swallowed a lump that seemed to form in his throat. Then he cleared his voice and continued. "The pastor here, and some of the men that he'd gotten together from the mining camp built on the foundation of our family's home. I didn't find out until the day after our wedding, when Pastor Lamb enlisted the marshals who'd come to help continue the build."

Joy's eyes widened. "You've known for days and didn't say a word? Is that where you've been spending your days lately, coming back all tired?"

He nodded. "It was finished last night, but I wanted to let things settle a bit and check it again this morning before bringing you all in. The house has been completely restored. It looks pretty much exactly the same as it did when I grew up there. Natalie and Nathan will love it, because it'll feel like home. It is home, after all."

As they turned the bend, the house came into view. It stood in the middle of a field, a little ways off the road. A good sized, whitewashed farmhouse with a metal roof, fresh with a lightning rod on top of it. They pulled up to the house and Natalie and Nathan grew all the more excited, asking to get down from the wagon immediately. As soon as they were set on the ground they went running toward the house. Pastor Lamb followed them.

A big red ribbon decorated the front door. Joy couldn't stop blinking. It was beautiful and like a dream. Though she didn't mind living in the upstairs area of the jailhouse, it was going to be something else to get to spread out into a home of this size, especially for the children. "This will be our house?"

His hands on her waist to help her down from the cart, Jack nodded. "It is."

She couldn't help but look at it and feel her heart swell in her chest. Mrs. Bolling passed them and took the basket toward the house. "I'll get lunch ready."

Joy nodded, but her eyes couldn't leave the big red ribbon on the door.

"I even put up a Christmas tree in the living room already for the children. We can move their stockings to the fireplace and they can even go back to sleeping in their old room again."

"It's perfect," Joy said, feeling a lump forming in her own throat.

The children came running back out of the house with Pastor Lamb in tow, looking sad. Natalie came running up to Jack, "Where's mommy? She's not here."

Nathan stood behind her asking the same question.

It broke Joy's heart into pieces listening to the children. For as long as she'd been in Virginia City, they'd not once asked about their mother. Jack knelt down and held their hands in his.

"Remember when I told you that mommy went on to heaven, and someday you'll see her again, but not until after a long time?"

Nathan frowned. "But it's been a long time."

Jack nodded. "Yes, but it's going to be a longer time. Meanwhile, Aunt Joy and I will take care of you and love you and make sure that you are safe until you get to see your mommy again, all right?"

Nathan continued to frown but nodded. Natalie swiped the tears from her eyes but said, "All right."

Then Jack pulled them both in and embraced them for a long moment. "I love you," he said softly.

Joy knelt down and hugged them both, too. "I love you both too," she whispered, trying to console them as best she could.

When the twins broke from their embrace, they smiled at them both and Natalie asked, "Do we get to stay here now, like Pastor Lamb said?"

Jack nodded. "Yes."

"Yay!" Nathan shouted, and they both took off at a run toward the house again.

It warmed Joy's heart that the children seemed to understand and at least felt comforted enough to move forward. Jack took hold of her hand, and they started toward the house together. The wind blew and flurries started to fall again, reminding Joy that she'd need to warm up the soup she'd made. "Do you think the stove will work?" She asked.

"I know the stove works," Jack answered, squeezing her hand in his. "You have nothing to worry about. We are safe here and you never have to worry about things from your past again. We have a future to look forward to."

Joy smiled, her chest feeling so full, she thought

her heart might burst. Everything was all right now —she was safe. And her Christmas miracle had come in the form of Jack, her marshal. She made her way up the steps of the front porch and reached out for the doorknob when Jack gripped her hand a little harder and pulled her toward him. She gasped in surprise at the playful look on his face as he scooped her up into his arms. "What are you doing?" she asked.

"Carrying you over the doorstep."

She laughed. "We've been married for a week, and you already did that on our wedding day."

He shrugged with her in his arms. "Well, this is a new threshold, and the start of our new life together. It seems fitting."

Giggles continued to bubble up in her. "It does seem fitting, doesn't it," she said as she wrapped her arms around his neck and pulled him toward her.

Leaning in, he pressed his lips against hers, and tingles ran down all her limbs as warmth pooled in her belly at his kiss. He deepened it, and she pulled off his hat with one hand and ran her other fingers through his hair. When he pulled away, he set his forehead against hers and their breaths intermingled. "I love you, Joy," he whispered.

"I love you, too, Jack." They met each other's eyes

and felt giddy all over again. "Merry Christmas," she said.

"The best Christmas I could have ever imagined," he said, and stepped over the threshold.

THE END

ABOUT THE SERIES

Ready for the next book? Don't miss the rest of the THE MARSHAL'S MAIL-ORDER BRIDE SERIES

THE MARSHAL'S MAIL-ORDER BRIDE ~ Eight brides each find themselves in a compromising situation – and the only way out is to escape west and become a mail-order bride. But will trouble follow them? Good thing they are heading into the arms of a law man. All the brides have a different, stand alone story ~ Read each one and don't miss out!

THE MARSHAL'S MAIL ORDER BRIDE SERIES

ABOUT THE AUTHOR

P. Creeden is the sweet romance and mystery pen name for USA Today Bestselling Author, Pauline Creeden. Her stories feature down-to-earth characters who often feel like they are undeserving of love for one reason or another and are surprised when love finds them.

Animals are the supporting characters of many of her stories, because they occupy her daily life on the farm, too. From dogs, cats, and goldfish to horses, chickens, and geckos -- she believes life around pets is so much better, even if they are fictional. P. Creeden married her college sweetheart, who she also met at a horse farm. Together they raise a menagerie of animals and their one son, an avid reader, himself.

If you enjoyed this story, look forward to more books by P. Creeden.
In 2024, she plans to release more than 12 new books!
Hear about her newest release, FREE books when they come available, and giveaways hosted by the author—subscribe to her newsletter:
https://www.subscribepage.com/pcreedenbooks

Join the My Beta and ARC reader Group on Facebook!
I publish a new story every other month on average!

If you enjoyed this book and want to help the author, consider leaving a review at your favorite book seller – or tell someone about it on social media. Authors live by word of mouth!

ALSO BY P. CREEDEN

CECIL'S CHRISTMAS MAIL-ORDER BRIDE

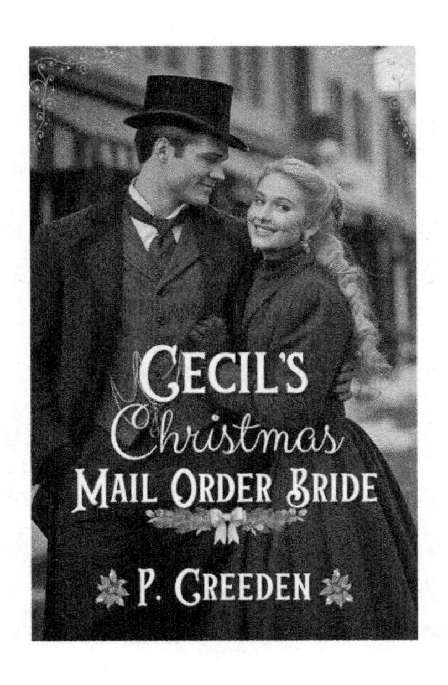

This Christmas, love arrives unexpectedly in Idaho Springs —by stagecoach.

December 1887 - When mail-order bride and nurse Gwendolyn Wright steps off the stagecoach, she expects a new beginning as bride to Idaho Springs' handsome young doctor, Cecil Cody. But Dr. Cody seems oblivious to their matrimonial arrangement. As snow blankets the dusty streets this Christmas, Gwendolyn discovers more trouble than tidings in this untamed town. Suspicion and rumors plague her efforts to bring holiday spirit and health to the sick townspeople.

The unlikely pair must learn to heal wounds and soften hearts for misunderstandings to unravel. Can unexpected Christmas magic spark love's flame between a man with no bride and the woman who has traveled so far to win his wary affection?

This is a clean, wholesome, standalone novella written from a Christian worldview. It has a happily ever after and features down-to-earth characters with real world problems who overcome them by grace and love.

Get your copy of Cecil's Christmas Mail-Order Bride!

And check out the rest of the books in the Historical Western Holiday Romance Series!

FIRST CHAPTER OF CECIL'S CHRISTMAS MAIL-ORDER BRIDE

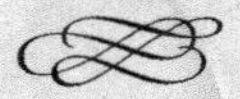

Cecil Cody opened the door of his clinic to allow his mother to walk through before grabbing her steamer trunk from behind her and rolling it out the door before pulling it shut.

"I wish you could stay longer, Mother. Two weeks was not nearly long enough," he said as he helped her down the steps of the wide wooden porch before going back to get the trunk again.

His mother lifted a brow. "Do you really? You're much too busy, and I felt that I was getting in your way more than anything. After all, I don't know enough about nursing to be of any real help to you."

"I haven't had time to send out an advertisement to bring a nurse in. I need to do that." The wind picked up again, bringing with it a bit more chill than Cecil had prepared for. He rubbed his arms for warmth.

Pulling the collar of her jacket up closer to her chin, his mother gestured toward his front door. "You're in such a hurry to get rid of me that you've forgotten your coat."

Feeling admonished, he bowed his head and stomped toward the door. His mother had a way of making him feel like a child again. He quickly opened the door and grabbed his hat and coat from the hooks just inside, and then shoved his hat on his head before swinging his coat over his shoulders and pushing his arms through. "Honestly, Mother, I wish you would stay longer. Even though I've been busy with work, I've enjoyed our meals together, and there's always a chance that my time would open up."

"Doubtful," she said, pulling her gloves on. "Besides, I want to visit with your sister, Marie, and her family in Denver for a while before heading back to Oregon. I'd love to stay with her till Christmas, but I don't think your father would like that very much."

"I wish you could have talked him into coming too."

"So do I," she said with a sigh, "But he and your

uncle have been busy with the harvest of grapes from the vineyards and will be barreling wine for the next few weeks. It's just not the right time of year."

Cecil mumbled under his breath, "It never seems to be the right time of year."

His mother laid a hand on his shoulder. "Your father tends to throw himself into his work, much like you do, since you take after him. It's as difficult for him to leave Oregon as it is for you to leave Colorado. We both would have wished that you could have opened a practice closer..."

"Yes, Mother, but this is where I got the call. The miners here needed a doctor."

She nodded and waved a hand in front of her. "I know. I'm just expressing a wish, not trying to nag you. At least you're nearby your sister now. Anyway, get my trunk, or I'll be late for my stagecoach. You will come down for a day or two for Thanksgiving? Your sister expects you to come."

Cecil shrugged but nodded at the same time. "I'll try my best."

"You had better. It's not as if you have a wife here to cook you a good meal for Thanksgiving, or every evening for that matter. You need someone to look after you like I've been doing the past couple weeks. You need to get married."

This conversation again? Cecil's hand fisted around the trunk's handle as he reminded himself that he truly was going to miss his mother though at times she could be frustrating. "I'll be fine mother. I just need a nurse to help me with the work, and I'll have more time to eat proper meals at home instead of trying to catch them at the cafe."

His mother pursed her lips and shook her head. "That cafe uses too much salt in all their meals. I swear they are just trying to get you to pay more for drinks."

"It's fine, Mother. But if it will make you happy, I'll ask them to go easy on my meals when it comes to the salt."

She nodded her approval, and then the two of them walked down the street to the Idaho Springs stagecoach office where they were already loading for the trip to Denver. Cecil helped the coachman with his mother's trunk and then, since he was there, he helped load the rest of the luggage for other passengers as well. Once finished, he turned to his mother, wiping the sweat from his brow. "I'll do my best to come down for Thanksgiving. I have more motivation, since I know you'll still be there."

"You had better," his mother said, resting a hand on his shoulder and leaning in to receive a kiss on the cheek.

Cecil obliged and kissed his mother's soft cheek. She smelled of lavender and powder, scents that he remembered from his childhood. He had thought all women smelled this way, or at least should, back then. Then she gave him a quick embrace before taking the coachman's hand as he helped her into the stage.

He withdrew his hat, hoping to cool off as the stage started to pull away. The wind pulled the sweat from his brow, but he could tell he still had more under his coat from the exertion of helping with the luggage. The sun still sat low on the horizon, and the rest of the town would just be getting up to start their day. He didn't know why his mother insisted on taking the earliest possible stagecoach out of town, but he imagined if she'd gone later in the day, he would have had a harder time seeing her off. Perhaps it was for the best that she left early. He waved toward the coach as it pulled farther away. He didn't see anyone wave back, and wasn't even certain his mother was looking, but it made him feel better that if she did look, he was waving toward her.

When the stagecoach was fully out of sight, he

let out a long breath. Then he unbuttoned his jacket to let the air in and started walking back toward his clinic. His mind was already reeling with all the things he needed to get done before seeing his first patient that day. He had a couple of appointments before noon, then he'd be heading out to the miner's camp afterward to see to the injured men he'd been dressing wounds for. A long day stared him in the face, but somehow, the busyness excited him and kept him on his toes. He was ready to take on the day with full fervor. But first, coffee.

GWENDOLYN WRIGHT'S FINGERS WERE WRINKLED, AND her hands felt scalded from the hot water that she worked with as she scrubbed laundry. She sighed and wiped the sweat from her brow. They didn't tell her in the Richmond Nursing School that once she finished the program, there'd be no jobs for nurses nearby. So instead, she found herself working in the hospital's laundry room. Sadly, she didn't even need her degree in nursing in order to work there.

A bell rang overhead, and even though it was distant, people immediately responded to it. Everyone dropped what they were doing and headed for the door. The shift was over. She followed them, wiping her hands on her apron, and flexing her fingers, trying to get the achiness out of them, and continued to do so as she stood in line. When she reached the desk of the supervisor, she signed out on her time card and then continued up the stairs and out of the hospital basement. After nodding goodbye to some of the other ladies who worked laundry with her, she started walking through the fading sunlight toward her home in downtown Richmond. The streets at dusk were full of people heading home from a hard day's work, as well as children running and playing after school and before dinner. Her stomach growled at the thought of dinner, but she just rubbed her midsection and continued walking. The few trees in yards here and there had empty branches, and she crunched over the dried leaves as she stepped past them on the sidewalk. When she reached her building, she sighed.

For the past year, she'd been sharing a one room apartment with another girl who was without family and earning a nursing degree as well. But the life that her roommate had been living was far different from the one she had. Having no family around anymore to help her had made Gwendolyn completely self-sufficient. Even though her family had left her enough money for a boarding house while she was in school and for her education, that money had completely dried up a year ago, and she'd had to look for other arrangements. Madeline had offered that they get an apartment together when they'd graduated. Now, Gwendolyn worked all day, scrubbing sheets and linens for the hospital, and barely made enough to pay rent and get by.

Her roommate, on the other hand, slept all day and then painted her face in makeup and went out all night. In some ways, it helped that they could hot-bunk. They could both sleep in the bed all to themselves because their schedules were so different. Though Gwendolyn didn't know exactly what Madeline, her roommate, was doing through the night, she had a few guesses, and none of them were good.

She caught sight of Madeline coming down the steps as she was heading up. Madeline's hair was coiffed perfectly in place, and her made-up face made her look gaudy and different. Not necessarily prettier, but somehow appealing. When Madeline saw her, she smiled and hopped down the last few steps. "I got paid extra for a job last night, so I bought some ham. There's some in the fridge if you want to use it in a soup for yourself. I just ate it as it was, but I know you'd probably rather cook it."

Gwendolyn's stomach grumbled happily at the thought of getting to eat something other than bread and vegetables. Her mouth even began to water. "Thank you," was all that she could say. Though she didn't approve of how her roommate was living outside of their apartment together, she couldn't help but wonder if Madeline was at least living a better life.

Madeline had more money, seemed to be sleeping more, and spending more time having fun. At least her joints didn't seem to ache, and her fingers didn't get wrinkles from being soaked in hot water all day. And then there was the fact that at least Madeline got to eat meat once in a while. Maybe it would be better for Gwendolyn to give in to Madeline's offer to start in her business. But no. She shook her head as she remembered the Psalm about envying the prosperity of the wicked. It wasn't that she felt that Madeline was wicked, Gwendolyn knew that she was not. But Gwendolyn also knew that Madeline was playing with fire as she went out at night. And that wasn't something that Gwendolyn needed to get involved in.

As she finished passing by her friend, she asked

God for forgiveness for her momentary jealousy, for her temptation to choose comfort over righteous living, and for the safety of her friend as she went out that night. Thinking of Madeline, Gwendolyn turned around and looked for her again, but Madeline was already long gone. She bowed her head and prayed for her friend again. Prayed that Madeline would turn away from her nightly activities and live a better life, and that she would be kept safe from the whims of those who might mistreat her as she continued down the path she was taking.

Gwendolyn didn't want to judge her friend, knowing that it wasn't her job to judge, but she did want to love her friend, and so she did what she could to help her friend survive while she prayed and hoped to live by example. But was all of that really enough? Was it the best course of action?

Didn't Madeline's mother admonish and punish her enough for the life she'd chosen? They were completely estranged now, neither of them speaking to the other, and acting as though the other was dead. If Gwendolyn had taken the mother's side, it wouldn't have helped, but just strained and perhaps broken the relationship they had together as it was. Instead, Gwendolyn had chosen to pray and love. She could only hope she was doing the right thing.

After she made it to their fourth-floor apartment, Gwendolyn took the hambone which still had a bit of ham left on it and stuck it into a pot with lentils. The one room apartment was a little chilly since the building hadn't put on the heat yet—it wasn't quite cold enough. Instead, the radiator sat cold in the alcove by the window, waiting to be turned on. So, she warmed her hands at the stove top while the soup warmed and couldn't wait to start eating. After fetching her bible, she set it on the table next to the newspaper so that she could study while waiting on things to cook. But soon after she sat down, there was a loud knocking at the door that made Gwen's heart jump in her chest.

Blinking, she stepped toward the door. "Who is it?"

"Madeline! I know you're in there, you harlot! Get out here with my money right now," a gruff voice said on the other side.

Fearful, Gwendolyn kept a distance from the door. "Madeline isn't here. I'm alone and will not be opening the door."

"Liar!" The man called out and banged against the door again. "I know she's in there. She was supposed to meet me at the club tonight with my money. I waited half an hour for her, and I will not be played the fool. Open this door now or I will make you both sorry for it."

The banging started up again, rattling the heavy wooden door on its very hinges. Gwendolyn clutched her chest. "I promise you, sir. Madeline is not here."

"What good is a harlot's promise? If I can't get my money out of her, I'll get it out of you just the same."

Now Gwen's fear truly took hold. She wasn't a harlot. She wasn't even certain that Madeline was. But was she? Gwendolyn couldn't firmly say no to that question either. But regardless, this man had put her in the same occupation as Madeline simply because they lived together. A lump formed in Gwendolyn's throat and tears stung the backs of her eyes. She swallowed it all back as she tried again. "I assure you, sir. I have no money."

The banging grew louder, and a couple of thumps hit the door as she could only imagine the man attempted to batter against it with his shoulder. Not knowing what else to do, Gwendolyn took her bible from off the table and hugged it to her chest. Then she began to pray. She prayed for the strength of the door to hold against the man's railings. She prayed that somehow, God would take this man away from her door. But as she prayed, she also came to the realization that she couldn't live here anymore. This was the last night that she should live in this hovel like this. Obviously, God wasn't pleased with her living arrangement, and this was his way of telling her just that.

Things grew quiet outside her door for a moment, and there was a murmuring of conversation in the hallway. Had Mr. Miller from across the hallway put a stop to the man's railings? Curious, Gwendolyn stepped closer to the door and leaned an ear against it, trying to find out what was being said.

"Don't think this is over," the man growled right on the other side of the wood. "I'll return for what's mine."

Then he banged his fist against the door one last time, making Gwendolyn jump and back away a step. Footsteps receded and then there was a gentler knock against the door, and Mr. Miller's voice came through. "Gwendolyn? Is everything all right? Are you well?"

Relief washed over her as she came slowly back to the door and undid the two deadbolts there. She opened the door a bit and found Mr. Miller standing in the hallway. "I'm all right, Mr. Miller. Thank you for your help."

His brow was furrowed with concern. "I told him

that you have nothing to do with the business that Madeline is in and that you just clean laundry and can barely make rent. He seemed to believe me, but he wasn't happy about it."

"I'm sorry you had to get involved at all, Mr. Miller."

He shook his head and rubbed the back of his neck. "I don't know if you should be involved in this either. Madeline is doing work that's going to do nothing but bring her trouble, and it looks like some of that trouble is going to spill over your direction, too."

Frowning, Gwendolyn couldn't do more than just nod, as the lump formed in her throat again.

"Well, all right. I know it's not any of my business, but I kind of think of you like a daughter—since you're about my daughter's age. And I don't want anything bad to happen to a good Christian girl like you."

She swallowed hard and barely managed to whisper, "Thank you, Mr. Miller."

He nodded, waved, and disappeared back into his apartment across the hall. Gwendolyn's shoulders fell as she hooked her bible into the crook of her arm and set the deadbolts again on the door. Mr. Miller was right. Her feelings about not being able to stay here any longer were also right. But where would she go? What would she do?

Like the strength in her legs had completely run out, she collapsed into the kitchen chair and set her bible down on the newspaper sitting in front of her. Bowing her head, she closed her eyes and prayed, tears seeping from her eyes as she did so. Nothing in life was going the way that it was supposed to. Winter was coming, and things would only get worse. What was she supposed to do now? She beseeched God for a long while, until she smelled burning. Her soup was ruined. She got up after saying "Amen" and swiping the tears from her face. Honestly, she wasn't hungry anymore, anyway. Pulling the pan from the stove, she set it on a towel on the countertop to cool before she could throw out the contents and clean the pot.

Then with a sigh, she sat back down on the chair again, her elbow pushing aside the Bible from the newspaper. There her eyes were drawn to an advertisement looking for mail-order brides to travel out west where there was a shortage of women. The office in Denver was looking to match career women back east who were well-educated to match with educated men with strong prospects in the west.

Pulling her gaze away, she shook her head. No.

She could never become a mail-order bride. That wasn't something she should consider at all. Heading off on a train to go meet a stranger... no, not just meet him. Marry him. She shook her head again. That was just crazy.

But for some reason her gaze was drawn back to the advertisement again. God often asked those who loved Him to do crazy, unheard of things. Was this His will? Was she really going to go run off to Denver, Colorado? It was hundreds if not thousands of miles away from everything she knew.

What was it that she knew? What was so great about it? She lived in a hovel with a friend who had become a lady of the night, and was pressuring her to become one, too. And even if Gwendolyn continued to refuse, it seemed that Madeline's life-style was having repercussions for Gwendolyn, as well. She let out a breath and pushed a flyaway from her bun back behind her ear. Then she looked closer at the advertisement.

Something sparked in her heart and she knew that she was being called to answer the advertise-ment. She let out a deep breath. "Are you sure, Lord?"

Then she rubbed the goose flesh down on her arms when they rose up. What a stupid question to ask the God of the universe. As if He was ever unsure of anything. She couldn't help but huff a laugh at herself. Then she took the paper and tore off the advertisement. She stuffed it into the front cover of her bible and then stood, turned around, and began packing her carpet bag.

A JOURNEY FOR LILY

When Lily Browne's father loses his job at the bank, he decides to make the journey out west, to claim land for cheap in Oregon. And when Lily hears of the need for school teachers out there, she decides that she must go too. There's only one problem. Even though Lily is barely nineteen, the wagon master demands that she cannot accompany the train without being wed. But she can't be a school teacher if she's married...

Wayne Cody became a felon by accident when he was fifteen. After serving his time, he was released to find out that he has no family, and no more than five dollars to his name. He doesn't know much about anything other than guns, horses, and cattle, so he attempts to get hired by a wagon train to help several families make it to Oregon to claim land. If he can somehow earn enough money, he can claim land for himself, too. Then, Mr. Browne makes him an offer he can't refuse.

Get your copy of A Journey for Lily!

And check out the rest of the books in The Reluctant Wagon Train Bride Series:

"The west is too wild for an unwed woman. If you want to ride on my wagon train and make it to Oregon, you'll need to find yourself a husband."

THE RELUCTANT WAGON TRAIN BRIDE ~ Twenty brides find themselves in a compromising situation. They have to get married in order to travel to Oregon on their wagon train. Each story in the series is a clean, standalone romance. Will the bride end up falling in love with her reluctant husband? Or will she get an annulment when they reach Oregon? Each bride has a different story ~ Read each one and don't miss out!

FIRST CHAPTER OF A JOURNEY FOR LILY

April 1854

JEFFERSON CITY MISSOURI

Wayne Cody blew out a long breath and pressed the barrel of his revolver under his chin. The late April sun beat down on him from overhead and the rock he sat upon was almost too hot to bear through his dungarees. Sweat beaded on his forehead and made a trail down the side of his face before dripping off his jaw. "Oh, God," he groaned, but was unsure what else to say.

He closed his eyes, his finger moving from the guard to the trigger and then he caught himself holding his breath again. A fly buzzed around his head, and he had the fleeting thought that the fly was likely to eat well soon. That brought other morbid thoughts to mind about maggots and other creatures that might find his body once he pulled the trigger. But when would a human find him?

He sat outside the limits of the town of Jefferson City, not too far off the main roadway, but other than the road, there wasn't much more than stretches of barren wilderness in all directions. It might be a few days before someone would wander off the trail far enough to find him. Would the livery keeper look for him when the horse Wayne had bought for three dollars showed back up at the livery? He doubted it.

Another breath expelled from his lungs; another droplet of sweat made a trail down the side of his face. A horse whinnied in the distance, causing the one whose reins he held to wicker softly in return. Would the person see his horse? Perhaps if Wayne waited just a bit longer, his gunshot would catch the attention of the traveler heading his direction. Then maybe he'd save himself from being eaten by whatever creature took a fancy to his carcass.

That made him huff a small laugh even though it wasn't funny. His heart rate had slowed. How long was he going to sit there before pulling the trigger? The steel in his palm was heating up from the sun blazing upon the rest of the gun. Maybe he should just pull the thing away, at least until the rider came closer. Somehow the thought of doing that made him feel weaker, more cowardly.

Or was he taking the coward's way out already?

Maybe. But would it really be brave at all to keep on living in a world where he had no one—not one family member to speak of? Not one friend. No job prospects, as a felon. And hardly more than a dollar to his name now that he'd spent three on a horse?

If only.

If only he hadn't drunk that whiskey on that day when he was fifteen. If only he hadn't gone along with it when Joe and Bill had decided to go turkey shooting after they'd been drinking. If only Bill hadn't let off a shot too close to the Reed's home. If only that bullet hadn't hit Mrs. Reed and injured her gravely. If only Mrs. Reed hadn't died before the trial started. If only those two brothers hadn't pointed the finger at him.

Then, maybe he would have been at home helping his mother around the farm so that she hadn't died two years before the end of his ten-year sentence. And prison had been hard on him. There were people who called the Missouri Penitentiary the bloodiest acres in the state. And they wouldn't be wrong. Only the strongest men survived. The weaker men ended up dead or enslaved in manners unbefitting to mention. Wayne had had to fight so that he wouldn't end up in one of those two conditions. Back then he'd fought for his life, but he'd paid for it in other ways. He'd lost a molar on the left side in one fight, ended up with a scar across his right cheek that had healed a bright shade of pink and caused that part of his face to sink in a little bit. And his now crooked nose had been broken three times. Getting employment had become impossible for him. With just a look at him, he was turned away before he could get one word out of his mouth.

"Oh, Lord, I'm sorry..." he groaned again.

The world would be better off without him. Living in the prison had been hell enough, surely the hell that was saved for people like him who took their own lives couldn't be any worse. A tear welled in his eye and slipped out from under his lid, joining the sweat trails to his chin. Or maybe God would have mercy on him since he'd only been in that situation because of an accident and an accusation, even though he'd been innocent the whole time.

Not that anyone believed him.

His shoulders slumped. And he could just about hear the hoof beats behind him. Time was up. He needed to go ahead and get this over with before he lost his resolve. Sitting up straighter, he took a deep breath and held it for half a moment, preparing to pull the trigger on his exhale.

"Cody? Is that you?" a familiar voice called out from behind him.

Confusion and embarrassment both struck Wayne in equal measures as his eyes snapped open. He yanked the revolver from his chin and stood quickly, wiping his face on his sleeve before spinning on his heel. He swiped at his face once more hoping there'd be no trace of his tears.

Sitting upon a chestnut mare, Mason Bradley offered a gap-toothed grin and pushed his straw hat up a little off his forehead. "I thought that was you. Didn't you leave the pen three days ago? I thought you'd be long gone by now."

Clearing his dry throat, Wayne looked down, dusting off his dungarees in a moment to gain composure. Then he shook his head. "Got no where to go."

Bradley's brow lifted. "Really? No where?"

A lump formed in Wayne's throat, and he shook his head.

"Why don't you come with me then? I'm heading up to Independence. My uncle there is a supplier of cattle and oxen for fools trying to make it on the trail to Oregon. It's easy money and he's always hiring a cowboy or two. I'll put in a good word for you."

Wayne blinked at the man and swallowed hard. "Why would you do that?"

Bradley shrugged. "I just thought with a mug like yours, even the railroad wouldn't hire you. Call it pity if you want." He sat up straighter in the saddle and reined his horse back to the road. "If you don't want to come, then don't come," he called out from behind him as he started trotting away.

His heart suddenly racing, Wayne pulled the bay gelding he'd bought by the rein to draw him closer and then shoved his foot into the stirrup and mounted while the horse had already started away at a trot after his buddy from the livery. Wayne barely managed to right himself in the saddle and shove his felt hat upon his head before catching up to Bradley.

Bradley eyed him with a half-cocked grin and nodded. "Ain't you glad that you helped me out that one time in the yard?"

Even though he nodded, Wayne's brows scrunched as he tried to remember. He and Bradley had always been on friendly terms with each other, but never quite friends. And Wayne didn't remember helping the man out, but it didn't mean that he hadn't in some manner. Fights were frequent in the yard, and sometimes he'd just find himself involved.

Regardless, as they rode their horses toward the northwest, Wayne sent up a small silent prayer. It wasn't much more than just a thanks. But he hoped that God, at least, knew what he meant.

LILY BROWNE SQUINTED OVER HER SPECTACLES OUT the window of the Independence hotel, trying to make out the shapes of the men on the street. Her father had worn his smart, gray suit and she had hoped to make him out by the color. Her spectacles helped her to read and to make out faces when they were close, but even her vision farther away seemed to be getting worse. She didn't want to bother her father with that small thing now, so she decided to live with it until they made their way out to the west.

A small cough came from the bed next to the

window, and Lily turned toward the sound. Her nine-year-old brother, Thomas, sat up from the bed slowly, his pallor making his eyes seem an impossible shade of blue. She scrunched her brows as she stood, setting her book and spectacles on the table before she came over, resting a hand upon his forehead to see if he was feverish.

"Do you think I could go outside today?" His eyes met hers, and his voice sounded a bit dry.

She reached for the pitcher by the table and poured him a glass of water. "If you're feeling strong, we could go down to the dining room and get you a bite of something to eat. And if you're still up for it, we can take a short walk along the street."

A broad smile spread across his lips as he threw aside his covers and took the glass from her. He took a quick sip and tried to return it to her hands.

She shook her head and pushed the glass back toward him. "Drink it all, please. It will make your throat feel better."

He huffed, but did as he was asked and downed the whole glass. This time, though instead of handing it back to her, he set it down on the table with a clink. "There. Now can I go get ready?"

"Of course," she said with a smile and stepped back toward the window to give her brother some privacy while he changed behind the screen. Again, she picked up the spectacles and looked through and over them a few more times, trying to determine which method to use when trying to see farther away. Finally, she decided that she could see better without the spectacles when trying to see as far as the street. Her brother shuffled behind her. He'd lost so much weight, his clothes were at least a size or two too big now. The sickness had taken away his appetite and how could her brother heal if he didn't eat well? Even though her father talked almost constantly about the adventures they'd be having in this trip across the Wild West, she knew their reason for going was two-fold. So that her father could gain land and employment, and so that her brother could get the air that he needed to get better.

"I'm ready," Thomas finally called out with a voice that was more chipper than she'd heard in the last few days.

"Okay," Lily said as she turned around, "but I want to see you eat at least half your eggs before I even think about letting you go for that walk. And a few bites of toast and oatmeal too."

Her brother groaned but nodded his head. "As long as I can go for a walk outside, I'll eat twice that much."

A smile pulled on Lilly's lip. She'd love to see him eat as much as he said. Together the two of them started out the door of their room and down the hallway to the stairs. If her brother could make it down the flight of stairs to the dining room without having to catch his breath, Lily would count that as a blessing all in itself.

A JOURNEY FOR DOROTHY

Dorothy Mason swore that she'd never marry again when her husband passed away five years ago. She just wasn't interested in her heart being broken again. But living in her old house in Tennessee kept breaking it by reminding her daily of her times with her husband, and she was having a difficult time letting go. So, her sister convinces her to get a fresh start by traveling west on the wagon train to Oregon. But once she's given up her life and everything dear to her and arrives in Missouri, Dorothy discovers that she can't move forward unless she considers getting married again.

Reverend Elias Stone doesn't quite believe in Manifest Destiny, but does believe in bringing lost souls to the Lord. With so many lost people moving out west in search of gold and riches, Elias feels a calling on his life to make a move in that direction, himself. So, he arranges to join a wagon train heading to Oregon and California. But before the journey even starts, he finds himself in a harrowing situation that could take his life, calling, and ability to travel away from him. Only by considering a marriage to a woman he doesn't even know can he continue, but is this really God's plan for him?

Get your copy of A Journey for Dorothy!

And check out the rest of the books in The Reluctant Wagon Train Bride Series:

"The west is too wild for an unwed woman. If you want to ride on my wagon train and make it to Oregon, you'll need to find yourself a husband."

THE RELUCTANT WAGON TRAIN BRIDE ~ Twenty brides find themselves in a compromising situation. They have to get married in order to travel to Oregon on their wagon train. Each story in the series is a clean, standalone romance. Will the bride end up falling in love with her reluctant husband? Or will she get an annulment when they reach Oregon? Each bride has a different story ~ Read each one and don't miss out!

LOVE WESTERN ROMANCE?

Join the Historical Western Romance Readers on Facebook to hear about more great books, play fun games, and often win prizes!

Printed in Great Britain
by Amazon